POEMS
STORIES

Also by Fairleigh Brooks

Fiction
Mr. Willy & Arthur
Notes of a Would-Be Astronaut
A Presentation of Short Stories Without Regard to
Marketing

Nonfiction
Beyond 17

POEMS
STORIES

by Fairleigh Brooks

To Lisa

POEMS

At Last

At last
at last
that broader sail is cast
and now
you know, NOW
its cloth so deliciously bosomed with wind

And now
oh NOW again
the sheer physics of the atmosphere
will not *let* you run home

Mark of the Question

We pass on with such holes in our wholes
a final cinder not equal to 2 plus 2 being 4 anymore
maybe 3, or just 2.78
Maybe not even that such sad state of arithmetic
finding us so very less than the parts we all once were

HUH?

We all
each and every one
pass in fresh and juicy
Wholes so 2^x greater than sums
x equaling at least 3
at least

What the hell happens?
No, really, what the hell *does* happen?
And why do we let this what
take root
take hold
drain us
suck us dry

(editor's note: insert big question mark here)

(no, bigger)

Leaving It to Beaver in a What-If World

Here's the deal about quantum mechanics
Mr. Newton and his insights from back then are not
     undone or negated
No, quantum mechanics merely hugs the Newtonian
     world
taking it in like a friend on a cold
windy day

And that's the deal about being a child
All grown up doesn't undo
untie
childworld
It merely hugs the if-then logic of kids
taking said logic into a world of probabilistic certainty
but that term is oxymoronic
Maybe probabilistic uncertainty, then
right Herr Heisenberg?
Ja, which is precisely the point
or, really, simply the point

In all-grown-up land
pony rides become a horse dash to deliver a serum
Runs of endless and borderless days …

become boxed in a calendar
yes, yes, oh yes
but with purpose, of course … sometimes
yes
The discrete nature of Monopoly
    36 possible results of dice
    1,2,3
    4,5
    and your racecar passes GO
diffuses into, heck, maybe getting what you want
or maybe not

Mother and father are now found in others
including one's self
if in ways not so certain as once was, sure
YIKES!
Yet in the new wiggliness and the sometimes
    approximation
close enough often enough
is a wavering electron orbit of broadness and depth
and the stunning dimensions that lie beyond the Lego
    click of if-then

Children Not in Dark

I was one of those smart kids early on
analytic, logical, interested in quantification
and yet as well interested in pulling off seamless creativity
    somehow, some way, some time
Anyway, you need to be eight or so to know you're you
and so at eight or so
having realized I'm me
I observed with my eight-year-old smartass brain
the adult world and its duplicity
their social graces that mask reality (but then allow for
    individuals to interact
the way atoms do in their outer valances, true)
their fairytale messiahs
the way they rip the artist from the child then don't kill
    it, but worse

And so in my eight-year-old cognition I said
"Hey, no thanks."
Keep your XLT Brougham 5000 and its built-in electric
    ass scratcher
later on
Keep your God damned Smartphone and the life you
    sacrificed to it
and so willingly

so God damned willingly
Wait, and you were afraid of those godless commies?
    HAH! What a laugh
        what a God damned laugh

Coming out of the very, very tail end of the Sixties
Reagan's inauguration removing any last vestige of
    grooviness
I was informed thusly:

    If you choose a non-conformed life expect one of two
    outcomes. Either you'll be very lucky, and your path
    will provide what you need and want. Or, you'll have
    a head-on collision with reality, and reality will win.

Look out, look out! CRASH BANG BAM!

KA BOOM!

Oh yeah!

I now must look back six decades to spy so distantly
that cheeky eight-year-old
And now after the crash and crunch
the metal squeezing in
the glass sharding out

I'm left with a John Chamberlain sculpture for a life
but, heck, that's OK
My own child is grown now, and she is an artist
    exemplar
her laugh is pure and honest
and I am the luckiest son of a bitch I know
Her parallax on life a seminal gift from DNA
her mother and me
later cultivated by her own self

And that eight-year-old scientist/artist smartass punk?
He's still around
grinning
battered
not only un-killed
but flipping the bird to the darkness of worse than un-
    killed

It's Right Next to the Pretend Good Food Market

I heard somewhere once the company paid consultants
  somewhere
fifty K to come up with the name, an equal number of
  alternating vowels and consonants
that flow and entice and are as threatening as mayonnaise
Or maybe 500 K but, anyway
consulting! What a damn sweet gig

Don't blame Walt Disney, for how could he have known
  how so irresistible
boxed-up experiences would be?
How could he have known how orgasmic would be our
  emotional reactions
to synthetic evolution? to the extent Amazon and its
  algorithms
wants to get our STUFF ready to ship before we even
  think we might want it

But anyway in this place with balanced consonants and
  vowels
is a stylization of café society
Inside is a modern take on that mid-century American
  blueprint of endless bright and sunny

inside is food programmed to evoke authenticity
canned chowder
inside holds an air suggestive of a culture
Say, did you see that movie about those people who did
    that thing in that place? Awesome!
Google Beat poetry, cat – in here the Wi-Fi is free
Inside? Music white people might call jazz
it ain't Mingus

Yes, we are that predictable
we have been for quite some time
But now the tech is in us like termites
every move we make
every breath we take
e(1)v(10)e(11)r(100)y(101)(110)k(111)
e(1000)y(1001)s(1010)t(1011)r(1100)
o(1101)k(1110)e(1111)
noted
stored in some cloud
No longer ours, forevermore theirs

Sometimes x = x, That's All

Robert Frost said, "Forgive, o Lord, my little jokes on
     Thee
and I will forgive thy great big one on me."
Hallelujah, brother

The last few days
hot
Across this summer
hot hot
our molecules expand
and I do think we all sometimes mingle with one another
molecularly speaking
as we go through our high-sun days

Simply by this expanded proximity you might inhale
     some of what I just exhaled
and yes, the sweat of sex

Today, then, is the first day in this season I have tossed
     myself naked into the universe
to see what's what
Or maybe just to see what's what

Oh, tossing oneself naked into the universe is not for
     everyone

Jesus, it's terrifying!
But for those of us who do
I think we search for meaning … well, come on, of
     course that
still, we're out there
knowing it will be harsh
knowing it will be stripped
knowing it will be cold and hard
and yet without, possibly, Thy great big joke

The Awareness of Self-Awareness

Afternoon
big light
yet sleepy
sleepier
sleep

Awake
later later
How Long?
dark
full dark, that's how long

Wait, HUH?

Question:
That tired?
Or maybe reality was annoying for a while

Day 24,585

You know you're grown up
when aching nostalgia for back then
is gone
when you understand you did not leave it
it left you
alone
hollow
bewildered
yet somehow new and fresh
able to accept and work
with what will come

You know you're grown up
when you understand you're not just
a tribal member
a nation's citizen
a religious believer
you're also simply one being in the universe
and that state is both enough and all

What is Forgotten About Childhood, About Children

Children go to dark places
in mind and imagination
On days with too many clouds
and no leaves
Warmer days, often, or less cold
coming after a run of winter winter
Still, days with wind like teeth
that nip but don't bite

The best advice I ever received on raising children:
    Always be glad to see them
Ain't that the truth?
For we cannot know to where they are headed
or from where they might be coming

I went to darkness
You went to darkness
We were ten or twelve
or nine
How did we survive such a solitary trek into _______?
at ten or twelve
or nine
And yet we did
and we do

The Halloween Thoughts of Buddhist Monks

Two days before Trick or Treat
beautiful morning, sun and blue
yet too warm
the TV weather geeks in their predictions – oh for the
    love of Pete
please dial down the perkiness, guys, gals – having
    burdened this Halloween
with a high of 81
so cancel the nip
the air will just have to get along without

Kroger invited kids to an early run with pumpkin
    buckets today
little skeletons and Wonder Women and real masks of
    CGI imps
employees made up Halloweenish, sort of
on the one to ten, most are three or four
It's not like anyone might have dressed up as Snowden
or Assange
BOO!

The monks live down the road a bit
in a Drepung Gomang outpost in the Ohio Valley, for
    Pete's sake
they're regulars at Kroger, an easy walk

unless you're American

They stand out, in the aisles and among the produce
in saffron sashes
almond eyes
But not so much today
tricking and treating in wine-red robes under those
    sashes
for today they are among apple arrangers pretending to
    be cats
and U-Scan overseers hoping to be Darth Vader's pool
    boy
and so maybe there isn't much difference, really, between
those such bemasked folks and our friends costumed as
    peacemakers seeking divinity
on this today, anyway

Kind of funny, I guess
that Bill Shakespeare was right
all a stage
we but actors
And, so, well … anyway, it's the Great Pumpkin, Charlie
    Brown

Longitudinal

On the day you are born a distant wave forms for you
and all those born with you
Across early years the wave moves towards you
moving with complete invariability

When your wave is near enough
but still with other waves, older waves before
you must already be on the shore

Then as your wave becomes next
you must step onto the part of the beach already wet
the part that will accept your footprints
the part the wave before yours has erased
of the footprints made by those for whom the previous
    wave was formed

You will stand naked
and pressed against the bodies born with you
You will let your wave wash over you
as this wave's time link converges with your path and
    those of your birth kin
Then you must leave
your footprints erased for those just behind
the very next wave being theirs

If late to the shore you can still go
no person or authority or power or thing will stop you,
    or cares to
you are free to try this new now, completely free and
    welcome

Your presence at the wrong wave
will have no bearing on those for whom this wave is the
    right wave, their wave
you will rob from them nothing physical or chemical or
    nuclear or alchemic
so don't worry about them, no*

*for you are already a footnote

Next Stop Train Village

When the lens of reality knocks on your door
or maybe simply sends itself in a plain brown box
(and you will open the box 'cause why shouldn't you)
what a day that delivery day will become

How shocking
unnerving
disorienting
anxiety-inducing
will depend on just how long ago you veered off the
    unquestioned rails many
maybe most
seem to always be on for always

and onto the rails of the HO village built between your
    ears
when you were thirty-two
or twenty-six
or nineteen

or twelve

Yep

How shocking indeed

will depend in just how long you've been inside a
    Twilight Zone script
you wrote for yourself somewhere between those same
    two ears
The signpost up ahead?
Train Village
Population 1

OK, maybe 2
'cause also in Train Village is the girlfriend you never had
not the one you did have
OK, 3, then – that best friend
the one never had at all

The lens of reality doesn't speak, of course, for it is a lens
    and is about light
you are dragged into its focal plane
allowing sight of insanity, however quiet
should you remain in Train Village
should you continue to live in a plastic beige house four
    inches tall with a green roof
and attend the red plastic school with that gossamer best
    friend
And look at trees, some forever in summer
others always in autumn

Still, Train Village holds childhood
or, hell, a sort of childhood, anyway

static
utterly stylized
dimensionless, really

In Train Village is a time that never really was
which holds a stick-figure life that never really happened
Which holds a life of dimensions not happening now
right now
In Train Village the joie de vivre of children is imagined
the deliciousness of their implicit abandon tasted,
     smelled
smeared across id and ego
In Train Village some mind penis is yanked
into emotional masturbation
What was *the* girlfriend's name?
Hers, not the other one's
Laura?
Katy?
Becky?
And the best friend's name?
Mike?
Tony?
Bradley?

Be thankful when the lens of reality knocks
amid melancholy and yearning
with its intention to shake you from an infinite warm
     bed

Yes, grit your teeth and be thankful
train villages
after all
should have a population of zero

REWIND!

The past
YEAH, BABY!
is like your dog's favorite stuffed bunny
the outside one – just Bunny
the inside one is Bunbunny
Bunny's fur is muddy-puddles stained
clumped into hard peaks after enough sun
left front leg gone
the stump hemorrhaging stuffing slowly
yet now long enough to bring flatness to Bunny's body
A Warner Brothers touch of the coyote? Tread marks?
    Why not
imagined, sure, or otherwise

None of these wear and play details matters to Dog
for her Bunny is the familiar
a constant
a dog's time machine that conjures dogpast
and so then humanpast

The problem with the past is a rather quick loss of
    resolution
quick BING **FLASH**
Soon mostly the good is remembered
and then soon so soon again

only the good is remembered
A yearning emerges from this faceted recall
for a time that never really was
for a life that never really happened
And in our backwards walkabout
DIDGERIDOO, BABY!
we carry our under-stuffed bunnies as artifacts and icons
that will open mind portals to way back when
And by the time we die we'll believe we were laid at
    thirteen
OH YEAH, BABY!
that we never spent countless Saturday nights alone in
    our rooms save for The Beatles
GOO GOO G'JOOB, BABY!
And, say, didn't we go to Woodstock? Well we sure did!
Yasgur's farm was groovy, baby, groovy to the max!

So, like I've never TikToked, or whatever
but that won't stop me from flapping my muddy bunny
    in my teeth and saying through them,
"Hey kids! Let me tell you 'bout 2-9-64
the night of the Fab Four's first appearance on *Ed
    Sullivan* – live, you see
That night was the happeningist happening that ever
EVER
happened."
Baby shook it up! We all shook it up and took the night
    train to The Future yeah yeah yeah

5G? I Phone 15? Well, sure, but listen
see, man, we bolted these tape decks under our
        dashboards and stuck these plastic cartridges in
yeah yeah yeah
And so the cartridges held a loop of quarter-inch
        magnetic tape with EIGHT freakin' tracks
and we could listen to entire albums, man, right in our
        cars! In stereo! Yeah and—
What's that? Satellite radio? Spotify? USB ports?
No, no we didn't have those. But see, these cartridges—
Oh, you've got to get your self-esteem measured? You
        might be low? I'm sorry to hear that
Do you have, like, a dipstick?

Hey look, next time I'll tell you about Kubrick and
        2001. It was so far out, man, so far out
And Patrick McGoohan in *The Prisoner*. See, it's about a
        spy who resigns
but his superiors won't let him
They send him to this island village populated by—
Well, I don't know if it's like *Game of Thrones*
I mean, I've never seen *GoT*. *GoT* is not Bunny, for me
but I guess will be someday, for you

Maybe Bunny is the sum total of our human experience
How many Southerners are needed to change a light
        bulb?
Five. One to change the bulb and four to sit around and

talk about how nice the old bulb was
It's OK – I can tell that joke because I'm a Southerner
    and I've read Faulkner
Consider
The last original *Leave it to Beaver* episode was broadcast
    on June 20, 1963
four days later Beaver and gang entered syndication
they never left this endless loop
Season six, episode thirty-nine today
season one, episode one tomorrow
shake that bunny
SHAKE IT UP, BABY! NOW!
TWIST AND SHOUT!
June and Ward and Wally and The Beav and Eddie and
    Larry and Lumpy and Gilbert
and Miss Landers and Judy and Ishmael
no, wait, sorry wrong story
Anyway, all these Mayfielders
Mayfieldians?
Mayfieldites?
Well, whatever the demonym they've all gone on from
    back then to just now
right now, this very moment
digitized for preservation

Digital technology
ain't it grand?
The whole of creation and all of life

depicted with 1
or 0
on or off
signal or no signal
something …
or nothing

Which means not a reason exists to prohibit one's own
        digital insertion
into the Cleaver household
Sure
who wouldn't want to watch *Leave it to Cody*?
or listen to John, Paul, George and Abigail?
yeah yeah yeah

Oh yeah, digital reality will be the final commodification
        of life
'cause it will be exactly that

Indeed
When the app for living becomes better than analog life
how will we get anything done
especially with Bunny between our teeth?
The lure and anticipation of fixing childhood perceived
        as broken
or just broken
the dopamine of that emotional masturbation
will become the ultimate commodity

and we will believe we were laid at thirteen because, now,
     that encounter is true
or true enough
even if just enough
And we will believe we saw Richie Havens open
     Woodstock
after all, we were there
or, now, we were

Bunny is nothing new, of course
Bunny is in every whitening toothpaste
in the weight-losing meal plan
in every little blue pill
in our messiahs
Truth is I guess we would lose our minds without Bunny

Flebermoshigosh! Woah, Brunhilda, I've lost my mind
my underpants are on backwards
And so we lose our minds even with Bunny, if we let him
and we do
Yes, we do, don't we
He takes us to a July afternoon
when doing nothing at all is in fact the something of
     what we're doing
but it's an analog nothing, not a digital nothing
and so it is something
and extraordinary in its ordinariness

Dogs 'n' Cats 'n' Humans

Cat/Dog

Cat flicks and runs away, just, oh just not too far, just
  right now

Dog wags and runs in – DUDE! – stopping only because
  zero inches

are between Dog and me

Cat has found the halfway of escape and halts to ask
  want some kitty?

Dog paws my leg

The moment Cat sees me seeing his question he answers

Well, you can't have any ZOOM AWAY

Dog has no questions, only desire to get what might have
  been given to Cat

Cat is sarcastic

Dog can't spell it

Cat would never buy a convertible

Dog would never put the top up

Cat might come to my funeral. Maybe

Dog would lie on my grave for three days and three
  nights

Cat could conceivably dispense usable psychological
  advice,

but in a way so condescending being arrested in
  development is better

Dog says *I will be your friend, friend*

Cat reminds me of my high school guidance counselor

Dog is my copilot

Cat/Me

CAR DOOR! CAR DOOR! C'mon Cat, he's home he's
    home! He didn't leave us!

I seem extra happy, so I'm gonna wag in circles. Back
    and forth just isn't enough

Don't much know, don't much care. Actually, don't care
    at all

But what if it's not him? It wasn't once, you know. That
    short one

who smelled like a sump pump borrowed his car once
    and OH BUT IT IS HIM! LOOK!

C'mon Cat. No, don't run away. Do you have to play
    that game? It's really pretty stupid

you know

He doesn't know my nose is one hundred thousand
    times more sensitive than his

Sniff sniff. Hey, you ate a cheeseburger four hours ago.
    Where's mine?

Oh well and yeah right there under my ruff and now
    behind my ears

YEAH! YEAH! YEAH that's it

Please don't scratch my magic spot and make my leg
    thumpythump

It's embarrassing. Cat sneers at me and ha-has

Did I eat any poop today? Well, not much, I guess
O.K. Glad you're home. I'm going to scratch my face on
    the sofa corner now
And hey! Thanks for naming me Furball XL-5. That is
    such a FREAKIN' cool name
Don't ever die

Dog/Me
Oh. He's home
Like that's news, since Dog's been twirling that thing
    since the car door shut
that's it Dog, run to the door like you have no integrity
like you could even spell it
You know, Dog, he's walked out that door ten thousand
    times
he's come in ten thousand times
He comes back, Dog, every time. Get it?
OK, here he comes. He's looking in the room now, and
    here's my cue to scat
Oh, Kitty Cat, where are you?
Jesus H. Christ in a chicken basket, that's what dripped
    from his brain one day –
Kitty Cat?
Hell, Muffin would have been better. Sneezy, Dopey …
    Cataloupe. Perky Pinky Pooky
but … Kitty Cat?
I hear his clomp, he'll look down the hall in a second
and … eye contact. OK! NOW! RUN AWAY!

I'll get to him in my own sweet time. Let Dog ingratiate
    herself 24/7
I guess I'll go to his funeral. Maybe

Act IV

In this place winter always comes before the calendar says
    it should
always a November day
almost always afternoon

Western clouds arrive low and textured with a rugged
    upside down landscape
and at first meander with the locals like any successful
    invader

Sunrays shift and refract and in turn form from the grays
    a palette
While altogether cunning and pernicious, this give-and-
    take makes the comfortable interesting

The day continues then
deskwork scolds imagination to return to random
    abstraction and sheer definition
School is dismissed and children return
the lucky to homes of listening, the unlucky to houses of
    hearing

The thought of summer is still yet close enough for
    darkness to come before many think it can

The persistent but not worrisome wind that delivers the
    clouds
its impatient gusts
knock heroic leaves from dormant branches into
    blizzards of red yellow
while sundown sparks hunger and the thought to do
    something about it

But before sundown atmospheric Visigoths crossed
the down-peaked cloud bottoms retreated into two
    dimensions
as that cover, now flat, stays low and pervades any
    horizon

The moment was observed by some, anyway
the lonely
the old
and the unlucky children

It's Always High Summer at the End of the Universe

In July there is a day, always
that spreads my molecules around like ice melting on
    rock
Sunny
Hot
The occasional breeze emphasizes the overall lack of
    breezes
and I flow into others melting

Who cares about clean underwear on such a day?
or borders
or saviors and deities
kings and queens
the worries of tomorrow

Now

So
in a way that concerns billions and zillions of light years
of joules and electron volts and quarks and spin and,
    who knows, maybe Nutella
minutes hours days eons seconds and milliseconds
bunches of stuff raised to negative powers of two, maybe
    even three digits
bits and bytes
of twists and turns and ragged rips in space-time

of perhaps even this sign

END OF THE UNIVERSE
STRAIGHT AHEAD

I'm there

Then

Lying on grass looking straight up
maybe I'm eight or twelve or seventeen or nine
clouds drift on
feathery birds meander through the fluid that is our
    atmosphere
mechanical birds poop out straight lines of condensation
the breeze announces not much breeze today
the wondering of what can this all be or mean

Right now

The end of the universe is whiteness
of course
what was prismed at one end is now re-prismed
Nothing is happening as everything is happening
the word *me* exists, but is without meaning

The wondering of what this can all be or mean
well, maybe nothing
but for the wondering itself

Tinkley Glitter a Go-Go

Apparently the whole enchilada is not only digital
but utterly binary
1 or 0
something, rather than nothing

In recent decades we have seen the Big Guy's box of
    Legos
spilled across the cosmic living room rug
Except maybe the multi-colored building blocks belong
    to the Big Guy's kid
Johnny?
Sally?
Billy?
Debbie?
Mike?
who knows
Maybe the kid's name is Constantine
or Listania Nova
or Gulf of Mexico
or Feynman Diagram
or $E=h\nu$
'cause any thoughtful person these days has thought the
    thought that maybe the whole enchilada
the whole shebang as far and as wide and as deep as we

can ever see or know
is simply and nothing more than the kid's science project

A blasphemer? Hell yes I'm a blasphemer. Jesus, you'd be
    crazy not to be

Big G god or little g god
Coke or Pepsi Visa or Mastercard Cheech or Chong …
    and most important, pardner
you want fries with that?
Whoever whatever whenever wherever whyever however
let's call the whole thing off

Mr. Newton's enchilada was simple enough
a tortilla, some chicken, some cheese
peppers and onions
nothing so complicated that we couldn't leave it all to
    Beaver

But then
BUT THEN
those Copenhagen wags had to start wondering just
    when *would* Larry Mondello's father
ever
EVER
get back from Cincinnati
Or did he ever go?
Or was he in Mayfield and Cincy at the same time?
And did he run over Schrodinger's cat?

And if he did was it on the way to or back from?

Was Mr. Mondello a particle or a wave?
Or both?
For how else might he have formed such a sizzling
    gamete
to impregnate a post-menopausal woman with the likes
    of Larry, for cryin' out loud
I mean, come on, the woman couldn't even figure Bruce
    Wayne was freakin' friggin'
BATMAN
And Lois, really now, over all those years you never
    caught on that Clark and S'man
were never in the same room at the same time?
Unless …
Wait, unless Clark and S'man and Bruce and B'man
fritzed around with quantum continuity themselves
I mean, dude, ya gotta wonder just what went on in the
    Batcave – I mean, come on!
And maybe they out Heisenberged Heisenberg

Yes, yes … YES! Now the clarity is at hand
the focus is resolving into sharp reality
Oh, you sly devil you, Mr. Mondello
you cheeky, cheeky invisible character haunting a
    Universal backlot
Cincinnati? HAH? I don't think so
More like Pyongyang

kidnapped by DPKR agents
black-clad rascals who emerged from a tiny sub named
     the *Bing Bang Whing Dang Ho*
which translates loosely as "the peoples golden cable box"
Yes, those ninja sort ofs grabbing Mr. M along the
     northern banks of the Ohio

The hapless Mr. M, then
never around for his younger son, never in Mayfield to
     say, "Hey Larry,
quit eating three 3 Musketeers bars at one time, why
     don't ya."
Subjected to horrible – yet perhaps oddly fascinating, it
     must be said – experiments
frozen for decades
then thawed out with a nuclear hair dryer found on eBay
     (fair price, but the shipping!)
forced to swallow Mentos and Diet Coke
the resulting volcano yielding none other than Kim
     Jong Un, a.k.a. Mr. Hairdo for 2015

This wacko circumstance then and also yields the
     unavoidable conclusion
(like we don't already know, Gertrude)
yeah, the unavoidable realization that CHEETO JESUS
     is really Eddie Haskell!
Yes, Mr. Hairdo 2016
and, Sam, don't you know he's giving America

THE BUSINESS

But then. What has the universe – all of creation, don't
        you know –
ever done to sentient and self-aware beings but give us
        the business?
Why are we here?
What's it all about?
Blah blah, blah blah, blah blah
I mean, how many one-and-only true ways can there be?

And so, well, so what if we're just Legos?
If a trillion gazillion blocks are snapped together in the
        right order, *then* a human being results
fine
The question isn't so much what this all is
or why there is 1, and not 0
The question is what could we Lego people
with the breadth of our questions and the depth of our
        answers
really make of 1?

Ahoy Fourteen-Year-Olds

God, you look so young
you at that end, me at this end,
we're on a Tower of Babel
and so how can I tell you what no one could tell me?

Still, I'll try
Pay attention to what's above your neck
there's nothing wrong about what's between your legs
nothing at all
but don't let that biological geometry rule your life
Plenty of folks want that thing
whichever thing it is
to rule you
They have found countless ways to profit greatly from
      obsession
desire
yearning
Deny them that profit
or most of it, anyway

Some of you know what you want to do with the part
      above your neck
and you know you know it
whatever it is is not resolved completely
How could it be?

But the image is clear enough
run with it
whatever it is, grab it and go
no matter how small you start
start

The rest of you need more time to resolve the focus
and that state is just fine
Make sure you're receptive to the signals from your
        subconscious
which are often sent not only hopefully but desperately
Start
then start again
Most of us do

If you see someone who needs a friend, be that friend
take the risk of being cast out
find the courage to defend your actions to those who do
        the casting
If you are friendless, unfold yourself some
expose a secret to the light of your community
the community the arrow of time has given you
Guess what? It ain't all that secret, not really, and it ain't
        all about you

Respect and cultivate your imagination
don't simply buy another's digitized world
or settle for a life of distraction – the golden formula for

    present and future fascists
There is no app for actual living
or getting your hands dirty

The imagination of homo sapiens
connected to eight fingers and two thumbs
changed
for better and for worse
the surface and substance of a planet
Take a step back and think about that
and then understand what we did to our home
the digital world is doing to us
Opportunity and tyranny are often flip sides
embrace the possibilities as you refuse to be quantified
a delicate balance, yes
but that is the blessing and the curse of self-awareness

Life is both beautiful and hard
nearly all of us seek to dull the hardness with divinity or
    chemicals
or both
In truth I do not understand the pursuit of the divine
although I acknowledge that honest pursuit in others
especially folks who have known despair and
    hopelessness to depths I have not
The chemistry?
Here's a quote from Dr. Mark Vonnegut, pediatrician,
    son of Kurt

"Drugs take all of your little problems, like having a
    difficult family
or feeling insecure, and trade them in for one big
    problem, having to have drugs."

Why are we here? Who knows? Maybe we'll never know
and, well, so what? We're here in such a binary way
for whatever reasons there is 1, not 0
That we are here, by the very observation of the fact,
    eclipses the why
We make that fact meaningful by "the breadth of our
    questions
and the depth of our answers," quoting Carl Sagan

You're fourteen
you quite possibly have sixty-six or seventy-six or even
    eighty-six meaningful years ahead
Smile, help, lend a hand
there's just no reason, none, to be a jerk

Create all you can with what's above your neck
and when you use what's between your legs
honor the newness
and commit yourself to provide the care every one of us
and all of creation
deserves
Smile again, help again, lend that hand again
and again
What else can we possibly do?

Continue

What if the end of Earth is not a sheer cliff?
The fall could be a stumble, however violent
down a slope likely very steep
holding knife rocks and tumble boulders
gravel swathes sucking enough and deep enough
to claim ascenders
But still not a freefall into infinite oblivion

Oblivion *noun* Middle English from Middle French
seminally from the literal Latin
2: the condition or state of being forgotten or unknown
Yep

One day, one sunny afternoon, within only a moment
that approaches with no clue of anomaly and then arrives
we simply fall off
Then bleeding from grabbing knife rock
but we have stopped Jacking and Jilling

The climb up will reveal a hatred of gravity
a growing acceptance of our fates
and a hope that, at the top once again
the day of our death is no sooner than tomorrow
possibly even a week from Wednesday

Un Mundo de Gigantes

Two Mexican women
no bigger than middle schoolers here
working at the car wash next to the Arby's

Kentucky is hot and humid in high summer
but nothing like Houston, New Orleans, Miami
or Tamaulipas
so there's that, then, for these two latitude adventurers

But winter
surely the two have known nothing like a real winter
zero Fahrenheit
a.k.a., -17 Celsius
and below
and well below, sometimes
Wind-driven drifts
black-iced roads
grocery store parking lots with piled-up mountains of the
    stuff
that can linger into March

What x in their lives was big enough and unknown
    enough
to make El Norte so appealing
Big enough and unknown enough to leave abuelas

    behind in space
and now in time
Big enough and unknown enough
to throw themselves into this world of white giants

They look happy
But, well now, don't we all

Un

My mom sits in a nursing home
like my un-vacuumed carpeting
the un-filled dishwasher that
when filled and started
will turn into un-put away

She drowns in time
her morphine my visits
I chase bits of time
grasping at some rainbow end of chronos
allowing myself to wonder about the orgasm of kiros
My morphine is a scavenged one half of one hour
but I'll smile with half

We prevailed over those godless commies
only to not prevail over ourselves
Jesus H. Christ in a chicken basket Pogo was righter than
    right
Observe
someone figured out how to sell us TV – we actually pay
    to watch commercials
someone schemed to sell us water
and now we pay to die

Have a nice day

Mildred and William

Day-to-day events making world history stole the youth
    from each
but more Millie
She waited sixteen years for this day
Bill some fraction of that number, his family largely
    unwrenched by Black Tuesday
But then his unit opened the Dachau gates
there was that multiplier – the utter depths of
    inhumanity, then
so Bill was ready, too

Millie in particular had endured sameness
going to bed wondering when
or if
a different tomorrow might come ever or otherwise
More than five thousand mornings awakening to stasis
or change making the news only worse

An edge made keener by enervation, and raging if quiet
    desperation
the ultimately indistinguishable itches of anxiety and
    longing
By skeletons still alive with eyes so vacant
they let some ooze from the backside of the universe leak
    onto this plane

Things go better with Coke

A quarter-acre of Earth
Cape Cod facsimile
The rarefied luxury of routine daily life now
reading the paper
eating dinner
food, then simply buy more
listening to the radio now
watching the radio soon

See the USA in your Chevrolet

The war children play on the floor
the post-war children awaiting their cues
All the children will be young enough to possess
gleefully and unknowingly
youth un-stolen
to not have a sucking shadow drop across
the coming volcano of fantastic abundance

Shake it up baby now
twist and shout
The Eagle has landed

L.A. Redux

So you go out to Los Angeles
camp a while on someone's couch
Hang out for a few days
and
if you're lucky
rain falls one magic night
and you awake to washed air
coolness and clear
When you look into The Valley
a flash between touching moments
let's you know the view on an elsewhere planet

When I was thirteen or so
I looked remarkably like Leonard Nimoy
Later
on L.A. trips
I looked less like Kirk's first officer
But
still
I thought
there must be a *Star Trek* script about Son of Spock
wouldn't a producer or casting agent
stop me at In 'n' Out
and sign me right then

right there?

HA!

The last time out
I stepped from the shower
I looked in the mirror
then at the door to confirm its full closure
then back at the mirror
"Hey moron!" I berated myself silently
"Nobody's gonna sign you to play Spock junior
or anyone or anything else!"

They drop me off at LAX
these people I know who'd had the guts to come out here
    believing it could work
and it did
Their goodbye is extended
but only the departing salutation is heard
The silent part is
"Go on back
to Kentucky now.
Stare at your river and dream of our ocean."

The corridors to the over-tarmac-suspended gates
are lined with palm tress
people from the world over
I long ago learned the script of a scowl repelling Hare
    Krishnas

they spot me
take a step then stop and turn

Eastbound planes first head west
towards Japan
We fly out over the Pacific
turning 180 about over Catalina
sea turtles always
The irrigation stops quickly
as comes Arizona, browner still

The green suggestion starts over Kansas
confirming east and wet
By Missouri we are fully there
the Mississippi soon vanquishing the doubtful
We've flown forward with the clock
into night
secret thunderstorms flash between and within
    cloudbanks

SDF approaches
or we it
or whatever
Flying over cars
and people who've never ever left
Jefferson County

My wife and daughter greet me
11:30 p.m.
85

hot sticky and the air smells

In a suburb here of columns and wainscoting
is a California home someone had the guts to build in
    the early '50s
this house has a mirror twin in L.A.
In the morning I'll drive by
think of some gone America
and wonder just how I would look
in pointy latex ears

91.9

A song on a way alternative frequency
percussion-based with singing strong and feminine
a voice I'd like to marry

This song peppers an afternoon of a day
making it one of those broadest of days
I am defined not completely
but well enough
And so not defined completely
but exquisitely

This day is hot
as the broadest days always are
The heat expands my volume, seen and not
I commingle with other human expansions, becoming
    connected by unknown alchemy

The light is green now
I push in the clutch and wonder about some life in a
    galaxy that
even when pulled through a lens
is only a dot so stupidly far away
and so stupidly far away
some bag of molecules rigid enough to give chemistry
    and sentience and, yes,

self-awareness
wonders about me

The Dog

When they came home from San Francisco that time
she was so happy to see them
They left her for ten days
a stranger in the house fed her and walked her

After her wag fest she ignored them for two days

There had been
there would be just one child
but Daisy put enough more into the equation
so that to the right of = really was a little family
Imagine that

Daisy has spent her dog life with them
and therein is the deal
and whether explicit or implicit has no meaning

She can see through one eye now
her left
trouble getting up
once up, walking
Along the hall for the bedrooms she moves against the
    wall as a guide
she is the embodiment of a being doing the very best she
    can do

and her tail is half bald

No point in getting the carpets cleaned until …

The secret of a dog is as a keeper of time static
On Sunday afternoons, in particular, he lies on the floor
    with her
strokes her belly
tells her what a good girl she is
sings her a silly song
oh so quietly
he made up fifteen years ago

Time stand still
while with her in those Sunday hours
the child is little again
wasted days have not yet been
dreams are fresh
unwithered
life, well, not yet brutal
Not yet

The Following Program Is Brought to You in Living Color on NBC

There is a certain past day
though fluid in that certainty
for while this day is likely in summer
the unlikely requires note

Still, just which season or angle of light holds the day
becomes faded in importance
by the simple existence of this day unlocked from
    memory
its skill in sliding through decades to now
today
maybe tomorrow

The day offers a sense of being parented
that is its sweet, diabolical siren
The day seems to answer *What if?*
but the question remains unanswered, always
The brave come to accept this whirlpool and begin
    resolutely to cage it
as they switch Janus masks

Cowards
so entangled by web
so befriended by yearning
slip between their sheets
with enough assumed
very assumed
certainty of tomorrow
a sureness fouling to efforts of carpe diem

What might be found in this magic day?
sharp angles are rounded out of their ugliness, enough
amorphous memories given resolution
Remember when?
I do now!

Lopsided friendships find balance, somehow
empty, so very dark nights filled and lit, sort of
Naked adolescent embraces happen without reticence or
     – him/her – at all
Mostly, comrades who might have born witness are
     there to do so, maybe

Sometimes Thinking Ain't So Great

Thinkers, some perhaps waggish, have suggested we are
     the eyes and ears of the universe
a way for the universe to know itself
How eloquent
how poetic
how hypothetically fluent, in some way or another

Douglas Adams was more precise
the meaning of life? 42
Perhaps Mr. Adams was even more precisely fluent
     because
in all honesty
I don't think he was joking

Heck, the universe creating an app to know itself is all
     well and good
but that leaves the app
i.e., you and me
up a creek regarding a way for us to know ourselves

Are we born unstuck in space and time?
Sure looks that way
for we spend our lives trying to get stuck
grabbing at repetition and regimentation

beginning with the first crying inhale once outside the
    womb
the smile of our mother, the plug of her breast

Mankiewicz and Welles were geniuses at distilling this
    whole shebang into a single word
They're 42? Rosebud

But then if one lives long enough
as well as thinks long enough (possibly too much)
well, hell, we wake up one day to find Rosebud doesn't
    explain enough
I mean, the night before, Rosebud – the external womb
    we spent decades chasing –
was so enticing and welcoming and we ignored the tracks
    along our arms
between our toes
puncture dots that connected into a picture of
    mainlining nostalgia
and the hurtful pleasure of melancholy

But now the next day's light reveals an existential parallax
    shift across the night
not that Rosebud no longer works now
only that Rosebud is no longer enough now
That womb world – one's own world, population 1 –
    became a prison in that next day's light
and that next day's light shone far enough ahead to show

the prison as asylum

And now life is in pieces, slivers and shards that will be
    put back
but only with the knowledge of jags and gaps that deny
    seamlessness
For in providing the universe a way to know itself we
    must break ourselves
and then put ourselves back
regarding a way for you to know you and me to know
    me and
42
for each to know the other

Maybe

Maybe you were
but I wasn't

Maybe I was
but you weren't

Maybe I am
but you're not

Maybe you are
but I'm not

Stranger in a Strange Land, Stranger in a Stranger Land

At some point, well, childhood ends
For those who have always looked ahead
childhood ends when those ahead years yield a harvest
	holding adult seeds within
For those who have not
the years of short and smooth
having failed to future
release barbs that spear into their now big bodies
The pulling out will be no delight

The more wrinkles and gray and ache the harder the pull
	but
well, at some point childhood ends
ends when the final threads of it are ripped ragged into
	desperate nothingness
ends when a world with a population of one becomes not
	so horrible
but too horrible

Approaching Null

Even those with the broadest and deepest, most enduring
      minds
with imagination neither lacking nor failing
who feel comfortable outside of comfort

Who do not pre-judge
or pull away from x because everyone knows y is the way
the only way

Who endure being spat upon to embrace the spitters
who know trees communicate chemically through their
      roots
who know, maybe, the state of Schrodinger's cat
and that we are made of star stuff just like that bag of
      sentient chemicals
who lives on a night speck barely lit in Earthly lenses

Even those few barely know diddly about squat
while the rest of us don't know even squat

STORIES

A Piece of a Morning Indistinguishable

The Cornerville General Store stands at the T intersection of a dusty road, State Road 32, and a dustier road, County Road 6. Route 32 runs parallel to the storefront, route 6 perpendicular. Ed is the proprietor, general manager, and often the sole occupant. He has been at his work spot, a rocking chair to the left of the entrance, since maybe eight this morning. Double screened doors cover the main doors, and squeak with a squeak a Hollywood foley artist could not improve. The broad pulls on the screened doors were a courtesy Rainbow Bread provided sometime around 1952, which was just about the same time the doors were last painted, Ed remembers. Joe, however, when Ed did that remembering, insisted the paint job happened after Eisenhower's re-election, "So we're talkin' '57, Ed. Spring. You know it's too cold around here in winter to paint. You can try, sure, but it won't stick."

A tulip poplar with a trunk diameter of nearly six feet at the height of a man's chest grows off to the left. Its lower leaves, some nearly as wide as a dinner plate, are dusty.

Sometime or another around eight thirty, on this present day, Joe pulls up in his 1968 Pontiac Catalina convertible, which he won in a church raffle in Nashville that same year. The odometer reads 17546, and so the Catalina has been around the block once. Still, a forty-seven-year-old car with 117546 miles on the clock could be considered low mileage.

"What kind of church can raffle off a four-thousand-dollar car?" Ed had asked Joe back then.

"They're Catholics, Ed. You know how those people are. They've got a lot of jack and a lot of pull."

"Joe, *I'm* Catholic."

"Well, then, I guess you know." Winning the car had been, and remained, Joe's finest hour. He's spent forty-seven years doting on it, and so the Catalina is in splendid condition. He receives offers constantly. One was $30,000, but Joe cannot sell his own proof of how lucky he was, once.

Joe walks from his car to the porch. "Mornin', Ed. Fine enough one, anyway."

"Mornin' Joe. Yes it is. Fine enough. Dry, though."

"Yep." Joe now takes his place in the ladder-back chair to the right of the screened doors. A tabby named

Tabby shows up, jumps up on the porch deck and then onto a hay bale, and now the tableau for the day is in place. "How 'bout I give you a dollar and you go in there and punch me out a lottery ticket."

"Now Joe."

"Well why not? The thing's up to a hunnert and thirty-six million."

"Joe, how much you got tied up in that game, maybe over the last twenty years."

"Well, I reckon somewhere in the neighborhood of, oh, two thousand dollars. Somethin' like that. That's all. Not so much. Not that much at all, really."

"Uh-huh. And how much have you won?"

"Well, I won five dollars last year, maybe."

"I see. So now, thanks to last year, possibly, you're down just nineteen hundred and ninety-five dollars or thereabouts, instead of two thousand or so."

"That's right."

"What do you mean, *that's right*? Is that all you have to say? Joe, what on Earth would you do with a hundred and thirty-six million U.S. American dollars anyway?"

"Well, Lydia needs two front tires, but then I'd splurge on four. And I'd get her brakes looked at. And, well, she's wanted to go to that Dollywood for the longest time now."

"Uh-huh. After that wing ding, what would you do with a hundred and thirty-five million nine hundred ninety-nine thousand five hundred dollars?"

He waits as the gears in Joe's head creak along. "The answer is five hundred, Joe."

"I know that! What makes you think.… Anyway, you couldn't do all that, not four tires and maybe brakes and Dollywood for five hunnert dollars. It'd be at least seven fifty."

"You're right, Joe. Maybe eight fifty."

"Yep. Hey Ed, remember when that Steve Martin fella was just gettin' big, and he was talkin' 'bout what he'd done with his money, and he said he'd bought himself a fur-lined sink? Remember?"

"I do."

"Now that was funny."

"Would you also buy a fur-lined sink, Joe? I mean, when you got back from Dollywood on your new tires."

"Are you mockin' me? Ed?"

"I am."

"Uh-huh. Well, just checkin' is all."

Thankfully the drone of a single-engine Cessna begins building like a giant mosquito at two thousand feet. "That's Willis," Ed said.

"Maybe not."

"Sure it is. He's comin' on down."

For the next five or eight wordless minutes the two watch the red and white airplane loose altitude and approach Willis's airstrip. "Nice landin'," Joe offers.

Then he watches a wedge of dust roil behind the airplane. "Sure is dry, though."

"Yep."

"He has a beautiful airplane. If I had a plane I'd want it red and white."

"You mean the plane you'd buy after the new tires, Dollywood and the fur-lined sink? And maybe brakes? And, yes, Joe, I'm mockin' you. What do you know about planes anyway? You've never been in one. The highest you ever been is the weathervane on top of your barn."

"I'm just sayin'. That's all. I've never met that Gina Lollobrigida Italian lady either, but I can still think about her, and I can think about the kind of plane I'd want if I ever bought one."

"You're a married man, Joe. Sixty-three years."

Joe's gears turn again. "You sure?"

"I was at your wedding. I'm sure. Besides, Miss Lollobrigida has passed on."

"Oh?"

"Yeah."

"You're wrong. She's still with us, I'll bet."

Now Ed and Joe are out of conversation for a while, as porch life goes. The store phone rings but neither moves, or notices much. Eventually Joe remarks, "I'm thirsty."

"Get yourself a Hires."

Joe gets up and says, "Think I will." He squeaks open the left screened door.

"And put your seventy-five cents on the counter, Joe. I mean it." He doesn't, but Joe does anyway. Whatever Joe's station in life, besides winning a Catalina convertible in 1968, he has never taken advantage of knowing the proprietor of a general store. The car is that sort of metallic copperish tan Pontiac had sported at the time. Black interior (not the first choice for a ragtop, but there you have it), air conditioning, power windows. AM/FM with an eight track tape player. Plus a screamin' 428 under the hood. A very sweet ride for the day and still sweet.

By now the time is 10:00 or so, late enough for the heat of the day to start building. Tabby is asleep on her hay bed. "Lordy it's gonna be hot," Joe begins. "It's already hot."

"Hot."

"When was the last rain?"

"June sixth. Morning, quit by noon."

"What's today?"

"July thirty first."

"Worse than I thought, then. You think God's mad at us?"

"Nope. I just think rain hasn't fallen for a while,

that's all Joe."

"A long while."

"Well, yeah, a long while, then."

"I s'pose. You know, my boy's boy—"

"Your grandson?"

"Yeah."

"Well which one?"

"Nate. No, um, Mike. Wait, it's—"

"Joe?"

"Yeah?"

"Is this about that intrawebs thing?"

"It is."

"Then you mean one of your great grandsons."

"Well now, I suppose I do, then."

"How old is this boy?"

"What boy?"

"The boy in question, Joe! For cryin' out loud."

"Oh, him. Eleven, maybe. Or thirteen."

"It's Cody."

"Cody?"

"Yes, Cody."

"Cody? I don't have a grandson named Cody. That's not possible. What would his last name be," Joe snickers. "Wyoming?"

"You don't have a grandson named Cody."

"Well OK then."

"You have a great grandson named Cody. And at

least his name isn't Cyril."

"You got a Cyril?"

"You know damn well I do, my great-grandson. Well, what about him? Cody. The intrawebs thing."

"Well now, he says the intrawebs told him we had rain a year ago yesterday. Two inches."

"That right."

"Yes sir it is."

"Wow."

"And I was thinkin'—"

"I told you not to do that, Joe."

"What? Do what?"

"Think."

"What, you go to that Yale or some such place? Is that it? You know I did put my three quarters on the counter."

"You did?"

"Of course."

"Well thank you."

"Anytime."

"So, now what were you thinkin'."

"You don't care."

"Sure I do."

"No you don't."

"I do."

"I don't think so."

"Well, all right, then. Suit yourself."

"You give up too easy. Always have."

"You're right. So what *were* you thinkin'?"

"Well, I was just thinkin' if we had rain now, it'd be good."

"Can't argue with that."

"But I'm also thinkin' it just might not ever rain again. Then what?"

"It will."

"OK, then. Yeah, OK. But it might not."

"But it will."

"Yeah, it will … unless it doesn't." A car passes and the driver honks. Joe and Ed wave.

"Who was that?"

"I thought you knew."

"Nope."

"Then we waved at a stranger?"

"I guess. If they're city folk they expect it."

"They're city folk."

"Oh?"

"Yep. Range Rover. You know, an eighty-grand Jeep. So, I was thinking Ed, when did you buy that '58 Chevy?"

"Nineteen fifty-eight."

"Now that's right."

"July sixth. And you know what?"

"I guess not."

"It rained all that day."

"Well, now ... you're right. A lot, as I remember. The down flow pond in the far pasture overflowed. We could use that water now. Especially if it never rains again, and it might not."

"Yeah, but it will."

"OK then."

After a brief silence Ed asks, "Joe, are you thinkin' right now *but it might not?*"

"Maybe."

"You're hopeless."

"That's what Lydia said. Just this morning."

"You should listen to your wife. Anyway, you're right. We could really use some rain. You know, they think now some dinosaurs had feathers."

"That so." Joe stands up and walks down the porch steps to reconnoiter the sky. "You know Ed, I think Willis might have dragged along some clouds with him."

Ed joins Joe in the yard, causing Tabby to show some interest but not much. "I think you're right. And not just a few. You know I thought things were getting a little dim like. And did you feel that? A breeze."

"It sure feels good," Joe says as distant thunder, gentle and slow, rolls across the valley. "Did you hear that?"

"What?"

"Thunder!"

"Maybe it's just Roscoe's bird cannon."

"No. It's thunder. It's thunder, Ed. Rain!"

"You think so?"

"I know so. I can smell it."

"You can't smell anything, Joe. You can't even smell you."

"Ed, I smell rain, and here it comes." And indeed a sheet of genuine rain is advancing down the distant hillside escorted by dark clouds high above.

"Look at that come. Glorious rain!"

"Just what we need. And it looks gentle. Well, gentle enough, like it might last all afternoon. Just what we need. A blessing from above, that's what it is."

"You might be right."

"I know I'm right. It's starting to come on more now."

"Yes! Come water come!" Ed smiles. Then, "Um, Joe, your top's down."

"Jiminy!" Joe walks quickly to the Catalina as the actual front moves towards them. By the time he starts the car and the top has whined halfway in place the rain comes down. The top touches the top of the windshield frame, then Joe uses four fingers to raise the windows at the same time, then he latches the top. Joe is only half soaked as he steps back on the porch.

"You're wet."

"It's called adventure, Ed."

"Well, anyway, I think you need a new battery."

"Ed?"

"Yeah?"

"Shut up."

"OK."

For many minutes they simply sit on the porch, enjoying the cascade and the pinging on the metal roof, watching the leaves on the tulip poplar being washed of dust. Tabby follows them into the store now, and Ed and Joe have lunch.

As they return to the porch rivulets run in the bare patches as water gushes from the downspouts. Soon wind-driven rain pushes them back into the store again. The day is dark enough now for a passing car to have headlights on as windshield wipers thrash water side-to-side. They look across the road at Willis's field and his airstrip to just spot Willis's truck bouncing and splashing fast towards the Cessna. Willis and his older boy jump out and brave the driving wet in order to tie down the wings and tail of the red and white airplane. "Was this predicted?" Joe wonders aloud, not really asking a question.

"I guess not," Ed answers anyway. "Willis didn't know, and he's on the ball."

"Oh, that boy's sharp."

Still the rain came. They watch the culvert along Route 6 begin to fill as a coyote looking for dry slips unnoticed into a hole in the side of Ed's barn. "Ed?"

"Hmm?"

"Do you think it'll ever stop rainin'?"

"Of course it will."

"OK, then. But what if it doesn't?"

... and Chris Davis as Rusty

When regular people think about the situation, should they care to, the opportunity is really quite odd. To be able to see yourself and hear yourself twice in each day as you once were. At eight or nine. If the ratings were good then at ten and eleven and twelve. To watch yourself grow from cute to handsome, but still cute. To hear your voice change and to know the world had once watched as you waded through puberty.

Yes, odd.

Not that you would watch twice or even once each day now, but simply that you could. Others, by the tens of millions, did watch twice each weekday, ten times in each week. They would watch two hundred sixteen episodes. On the morning of the day after episode two hundred sixteen had rolled viewers of again tens of millions, if perhaps of a somewhat different aggregate now, would start again with episode one, when you were eight again and watch, over the next twenty-three weeks and change, as you become fourteen again. Sometimes, because of scheduling or whatever on the BackThen TV network, episode two hundred sixteen would be shown in the 9:00 to 9:30 slot (EST), and then episode one would pick it all up again in the 9:30 to 10:00 slot. Bingo, omega and alpha just right there on the same morning.

Eight to fourteen. Eight to fourteen. Cutest damn kid ever. And could he act! Oh well, like any of the viewers gave a flying hoot about Chris Davis now. No, they cared only about Rusty Buster at eight or fourteen or ten and a half. They didn't care about mostly broke Chris at seventy-five, living in a one bedroom overlooking the 405, driving an '07 Focus with flaking paint, sometimes watching himself on BackThen TV at 9:00. Or 9:30. Sometimes. No, wait, yep ... too many times.

Oh That Rusty! debuted on September 6, 1958. The last show was broadcast May 5, 1964. Over six seasons it plodded along in the ratings, never breaking the number twenty position.

Syndication, however, was another story. *OTR!* was on its way to dusty forgottenness when, three months after the last show aired, the series entered syndication. For the next twenty years the show was rerun more often – far more often – than not, and since July of 1988 the show has been in constant rotation, never not broadcast on some network somewhere. BackThen acquired the rights in 2010.

Chris received a cut from the sale of lunch boxes and trading cards and a comic book series and the *OTR!* board game. But his agent did not negotiate residuals for Chris, nearly unheard of for child actors in that day. When his mother died he was surprised, given his mother's disregard of him, to find a large stash of merch as he cleaned out her house. He autographed each item and did well selling the artifacts on eBay for a couple of years. He was careful with the proceeds, but now they were gone. He banked his Social Security deposits during the eBay years, but now that balance was also depleted, so these days his income came from his ongoing Social Security and appearance fees from occasional nostalgia conventions.

By the end of the current production season in spring of 1964, even though the ratings weren't so bad, the producers wondered if *Oh That Rusty!* just might have reached the end of its narrative arc. Chris had finished his wade through puberty, and network execs were pressing for a color production, which would have jumped the cost per episode significantly, and while the ratings weren't all that bad, they weren't all that good. Still, they had been consistent.

The end of *OTR!* was fine with Chris. He'd spent a very significant chunk of his childhood on the set and on the lot. At fourteen now he was curious about normal, about just being a kid, and so he enrolled at Hollywood High.

At first he was somebody. Of course he was, he was Rusty Buster. And yet the tense of his status changed quickly enough, from *Aren't you…* to *Hey, weren't you…* to *Wait, didn't you use to be…* That final query contained *somebody* implicitly. Chris certainly wasn't the first star at Hollywood High, or the only one during his enrollment there. Patty Parker of *Uh-Oh, Linda!* was a schoolmate, as was Tommy Wilson of *Larry and Bobo* fame. But then Patty and Tommy would turn out OK. They both learned, or figured out soon enough, what success was, even continuing success. That it's simply a seed, and the germination of the seed and the care of the resulting little plant and it's growth are the responsibility of the person receiving the seed. Such responsibility can be no other's, ultimately.

Chris never really learned that aspect of success objectively. He did figure it out, pretty much, but too late.

He graduated from HH with some distinction, then enrolled at USC in philosophy, a course which Chris cancelled after his sophomore year due to his own internal low ratings.

Three wives entered Chris's life and three wives exit- ed. One child was produced, a son Chris hadn't seen or heard from in thirty-five years. By the time Brandon Davis was eight he looked just and exactly like his father, which is to say just and exactly like young Rusty Buster. By the time he was nine he wore sunglasses everywhere he because he had to. By the time he was ten he hated Rusty Buster, which is to say his father.

Reruns of *OTR!* were kryptonite to Brandon. He'd seen a few anyway, of course, including episode 5, season 2, in which Rusty becomes lost in some woods. At the 22:07 mark he's rescued by a ranger. (The ranger was played, somewhat as a lark, by Ronald Reagan. But only somewhat. Reagan really liked *OTR!*). Brandon rewrote the script. Not just in his head – no not simply that – he actually rewrote it, typing it in script format and binding the pages with brass brads. In the rewrite Rusty is eaten by a bear, on camera and with plenty of closeups.

And so from about age twenty on the pieces were there for Chris, but many were wrong pieces. Or right pieces at the wrong time or disjointed pieces which would never find a right time or mate, however disjointed in geometry and time that other lone piece itself was. In 1988 an *OTR!* reunion show was planned. The script was written and pre-production had started when Talbot

Montgomery, who played Rusty's father, Charlie Buster, killed his off-screen wife of thirty-two years. Yes, there actually is such a thing as bad publicity, even in Hollywood, and the murder – B-script gruesome – sunk the reunion. Still, Chris was under contract, which required a $50,000 kill payment, a sum still worth noting in 1988 when an Audi 5000 was twenty-two grand and change and the thought of a Bentley SUV was absurd and a place in Pacific Palisades could still be had for six figures. Not to mention the ranger who had rescued Rusty in those woods was president. Oh, not just of SAG at one time, no not just that but of the United States. Heck, a B script of life – you know, *real life* – imitating art with geopolitical consequences. And that's a wrap.

And sometimes Chris thought about Yvette Vickers, best known for her role in *Attack of the 50 Foot Woman.* In her early eighties she became reclusive, dying alone in her Holmby Hills home, her bills on autopay. A concerned neighbor eventually broke into Vicker's house. A forensic examination concluded she had been dead about one year, her body having mummified. Well, death above the 405 wasn't as so intriguing, oh no. Chris figured his neighbor, Mrs. Taylor, who had a key, would notice his smell, if not his absence, and investigate. Death in a cookie cutter apartment, even of Rusty Buster, didn't seem too newsworthy. Maybe in another locale his demise would make the papers and the eleven o'clock and the lead on home pages around the internet.

So, yes, there were the sporadic nostalgia conventions. Those events paid, but Chris had grown weary of them, and the surprise, if not horror, in the faces of fans who just never expected Rusty Buster to be an old man. The main facets of Chris's life, then, indistinct and with not much account, simply plodded forward as same days that lined up into same years, and so into decades. Indeed, the opportunity to see and hear yourself as you once were is, in point of fact, indeed so, so strange. And, in recent years now, that lure of Googling yourself yet another time, and then so many others beyond. And to read the *OTR!* Wikipedia entry and then the entry on Chris Davis, wondering who created the content and who updated it. Well, he still had fans, anyway.

Days without content would tick by and be over so soon, or soon enough. A glance at the evening clock sparking the wondering – spoken aloud – *How did it get to be 10:30?*

Chris had his favorite episodes, of course. Episode 11, season 2. In that one Rusty buys an automatic homework doer from his brother's friend Herbie Basham, who is a pediatric sociopath.

And of course episode 12, season 4, which finds Charlie in hot water with the IRS, thanks of course to Rusty. But Chris's very favorite was episode 2, season 4, in which John Glenn played himself. Although not part of the script, Glenn gave Chris a mockup of an astronaut's helmet. Even as a boy Chris saw Glenn's act as so genuine, and knew Glenn was the sort of parent he not only didn't have, but would never have.

Mrs. Taylor knew exactly who Chris was and she did watch twice each day, but she never let on about knowing Chris and Rusty were one in the same. Oh, he knew she knew, and she knew he knew she knew, and so on, but that she pretended she didn't know meant so much to Chis, so very much.

The two got together usually once in each week, usually Wednesday evening. Got together as neighbors. They'd watch an old movie, sometimes eat Chinese takeout. A Wednesday came and went for Mrs. Taylor with no Chris, or any word from him. She was curious but did not pry, but when the next Wednesday repeated the prior absence Mrs. Taylor became concerned. She called with no answer and knocked with no answer. He hadn't picked up his mail in three days, or checked his email in as many.

On Friday she notified the police, Officer Dakota

Palmer answering the call. He explained to her some people weren't actually missing, but had left behind their present life by choice, and so at this juncture he could not file a missing person report, not on an adult. Officer Palmer was a good policeman, having an intuitive nose, and he acknowledged to himself that something did seem off. "He does have a girlfriend, you know, believe it or not," Mrs. Taylor told. "A pretty thing, and much younger. I don't really get it, but then that's their business. Julie Wilson, that's her name."

"Oh? Do you have her number?"

"No. But she lives in Echo Park. Does that narrow it?"

"Yes. Enough, anyway, I would think. And listen, this will be, well, not exactly official, if you understand."

"I do. And thank you." She thought to tell the officer that Chris was once Rusty, but did not.

The next Monday Officer Palmer checked the info on the two Julie Wilsons living in Echo Park. Only one fit the age range. On his lunch break Officer Palmer stopped by the one Julie's apartment. "Mrs. Taylor is concerned about Mr. Davis. She mentioned you're his girlfriend?"

Julie did not reply right away, which Officer Palmer noticed, of course. As she was not replying she was thinking of asking the officer how broadly he defined *girlfriend*. Then, "Yes, I gu— Yes. I am."

"I was thinking you might have an idea where Mr. Davis is, then," Officer Palmer queried. "I mean, do you?"

"Well I ..." Julie began. Chris's disappearance was news to her, as they would often go ten or twelve days without communicating. She hadn't thought about his possible location, of course, not knowing there was any reason to do so. But then in a flash she knew she knew. She looked at the officer, who was looking directly at her in such an investigative way, knowing now she knew. Julie was uncertain about telling, wondering if she was helping Chris, or somehow betraying him.

"Ms. Wilson?"

"Yes. Yes I think I do. But look, I'll need to go with you."

"That's not poss—"

"I understand. But I must go along. There's no other way. And we'll need access to the Amalgamated lot."

"Oh?"

"Don't you— Oh, well, Chris, Mr. Davis, was a child star way back. *Oh that Rusty!*"

"Really? I think my kids watch that show. In the summer, anyway, on some rerun network. So, that would put Mr. Davis, let's see ... well into his seventies." Now Officer Palmer's face told he had assembled enough pieces, and that he too was pretty sure where Chris was. "But, look, I can't put you in danger."

"There will be no danger, not if I'm there. I know Chris. There's no other way."

Officer Palmer considered briefly. That he was acting more or less on his own was both good and not good. "OK."

Julie met Chris when he still lived in Echo Park. They were both post-war, sure, Chris being born in '50. But she was way, way post-war. In fact when she met Chris she had no idea he had been a beloved child star, meaning the kid who was Rusty Buster. In fact she had never watched a single episode of *OTR!* Golly, not even episode 9, season 4, in which Rusty traded the kid across the street – you know, little Sammy – for a go kart. Hoo boy, did Rusty get it that time!

She liked Chris, despite the age difference. It wasn't an intercourse like, but it also wasn't platonic, or some kind of ersatz sibling thing. And then, across one L.A. afternoon one day, intercourse did pop up like a clown balloon, and that coupling was simply and utterly remarkable for Julie.

But just that once. Chris hinted, quite strongly, that the next time he wanted her to wear a tartan skirt and white high-rise panties and flats and a blouse with a Peter

Pan collar and pull her hair back in a ponytail and call herself Mary Sue Roberts. She had to Wiki the collar and IMDB Mary Sue Roberts. When she found out Mary Sue was the main squeeze of Harry, Rusty's older brother, that was the end of round two, intercourse-wise. In fact she almost vomited on her keyboard. But, for reasons she couldn't discern, their relationship continued, and from that moment on *was* platonic. Or something.

The house – once a home for a family that existed in a script, and then on 35mm film, and then on 16mm for syndication, and now in digital files at BackThen and in box sets on eBay – that house once sat forty feet back from the fictitious Maple Street in the invented town of Mount Vista. Viewers never knew – viewers who assumed (because they wanted to and/or needed to) that the Buster house was in anywhere-they-needed-it-to-be, USA – they never knew that right behind the leafy back yard ran the Los Angeles River, a sad stream confined to a concrete culvert, its riparian habit not just denied, but denied completely in some miserable triumph over nature.

Long ago, after the house had been updated for *Betty and Bonnie* and then after that series was cancelled, the usefulness of the house expired. It was moved to a backlot. Clearly no longer a home, if only for scripted characters and their antics, it was now not even a house so much, but a sad relic that had passed some point of no return decades back. Windowpanes were missing. Cracks meandered in 90° angles within the stone veneer. The soffit between that first-floor veneer and the second floor siding gaped. Clapboards had fallen away decades ago, and the whole building had a vague out-of-plumb look and feel, some kind of monument now to what the middle class and its post-war shindig had once been.

The studio was off Melrose, a good forty-five minutes away by distance and traffic. Officer Palmer had contacted Amalgamated. They were to go to gate nine.

At the gate a guard approached. "You folks here for the Buster house?"

"Yes."

"I've seen him in here, you know. You know, Rusty. People come in here sometimes, come up from the river. There's a hole in the fence back there, so I've seen him. Rusty. Well, you know, Davis. Chris Davis. I mean, I think it's him. Pretty sure. I've never said anything, though. Seemed harmless."

"Have you seen him today."

"No. Saw him about, oh, maybe a month ago and– No, wait. Last week. I saw him late last week, right before dusk."

"A couple of days ago, then."

The guard considered. "Yeah. It was Saturday."

"And you aren't concerned?"

"Concerned?"

"About trespassing. That's part of your job, isn't it?"

"Yeah, sure. But I know Rusty wouldn't cause any harm. I figured he was here for…."

"For what?"

The guard did not answer right away. "Memories. I guess. You know, the good ol' days. And the thing is…."

"Yes?"

"Well, he was holding a helmet. An astronaut's helmet, I think. I could see it clearly."

The officer looked at Julie, then back at the guard. "Just where did you see him?

"On Maple Street. Where his house used to be. Or, I mean, you know, the house in the series."

"Used to be? Where is that house now?"

"In the boneyard. Backlot three." The guard climbed into a golf cart with a revolving amber light on top. "Follow me."

"Look, we need to—" Julie started. Then turning to the guard, "Sir?"

"Yes ma'am?"

"Could you stop fifty yards away or so?" The guard looked at Officer Palmer, who nodded. "OK. And I guess I'd better turn off my light."

Before reaching that stopping point Julie spotted Rusty's house and gasped. The place looked like tattered fiction, as if the hundreds of thousands of words from six years' worth of scripts were termites that continued to eat away at the walls and floors and rafters and joists. Remember episode 29, season 5? You know, when Rusty put his wet campfire wood in the clothes dryer? What a laugh riot!

The three approached the house, none quite sure what to do. They walked around back, the French doors from the dining room opening now onto a rubble-strewn slope. "What are we looking for?" the guard asked. "If you don't mind me asking, I mean."

Officer Palmer figured the question was aimed at him. "I'm not sure. Ms. Wilson?"

Julie wasn't sure either. The officer's answer to the guard and then his question to her did not seem professional, as though he was not in control. But then he wasn't, of course. She had led them here, to the remains from a once space age, to some kind of fallout from the New Frontier. "I'm not sure either. But I guess we'll see."

Back on the left side of the house now. The guard was answering a radio call. A movement caught Julie's eye, and then she saw Chris poke his head above the sill of a side upstairs window, in the bedroom Rusty and Harry had shared. When she looked at Officer Palmer he was looking back at the patrol car. Neither had seen him, and she wasn't telling. Not just right now, anyway.

Julie started walking towards the front entrance. "Ms. Wilson! Wait!" She turned to face the officer, putting her right index finger on her lips and waving him back. He complied. She continued, up the flagstone steps. The front door was gone, the tile in the entrance hall warped and cracked. To the right was the living room, where so much stylized American living had once upon a time gone on, gone on amid Elvis and space shots and with an optimism now unknowable. She knew enough about TV production to know the living had mostly gone on in the ceiling-less soundstage reproduction of this space, under klieg lights and boom mics as a child of reality played a child in a script and on celluloid, a production once so delightfully analog, yet now held in some kind of perpetuity as 1s and 0s in the digital files of BackThen.

At the bottom of the stairs Julie asked quietly, "Chris? It's Julie." No response. Again, louder, but still nothing. She heard Chris whistling, then after a moment realized his tune was the upbeat opening theme from *OTR!*

Julie was silent now, for maybe a full minute as the

whistling continued. Then, in a script voice, "Rusty? Billy Harrison called. He wants to ride bikes. But be home early, it's a school night. OK?"

A pause now, almost too long but not. "OK, mom. Sure thing."

And Thus the Baton is Passed

Knowing right up front that T. Peterson Armbruster was crazy won't hurt. Not *strip naked, climb atop the jungle gym in the playground and play Beethoven's seventh on kazoo* crazy. No, his looniness was subtler.

If only it hadn't been.

The first step that would lead to the eventual uncovering of Mr. Armbruster's jangled synaptic patterns, not to mention his pervasive inadequacy (a trait that would have existed even within sanity), began on April first. Two months and some days later the irony of the date would eventually occur to Walter Richardson.

During the last ten of his twelve years of tenure as principle of Susan B. Anthony Memorial High School, Walter had, on each April first, begun his search for a commencement speaker for the early-June graduation of the senior class.

In his first year he hadn't asked until the later days of May, never imagining that who might agree to speak less than two weeks before the ceremony remained available for a reason. Or even reasons, take your pick.

In year two he moved the search start to May first with not much improvement. But, still, some improvement, Walter figured, since most people held Will Roberts, vice president of installment loans at People's National Bank, in some higher esteem than Harold Zecker, the owner of the Sparkly Spray Car Wash and Bait Shop. To Walter's relief, the news two months later of Mr. Roberts' almost three-year embezzlement scheme broke on the same day the Bradford Street sewage pumping plant blew up, relegating news of the ruination of his choice of inspiration to young men and women to section two, page six in the *Daily Clarion*.

In more recent years Walter had convinced a former governor, an AA ball player, a sitting federal judge, and Lila Penney-Pearl, B-list Hollywood actress, to prod the kids into adulthood with smiles and hope, and with wisdom either conceived, perceived, or tripped over. Just three years ago, and just in time, he had uncovered the scheme of a man who was passing himself off as a third-tier Kennedy, replacing him with the son of an un-flown astronaut. The man was remarkably not too bad at all.

Had T. Peterson Armbruster not run for a city council seat, Walter doubted his pompous name would have ever sat in his brain long enough to reach conscious thought. But he had, and so it did, and so Walter had, in a quest for inspiring words, accepted quickly an offer from a man whose only actual accomplishments were two. One, coming in third in a three-way race for a city council seat in a town of 156,000. Jacobs – 3,251, Anderson – 2,304, Armbruster – 219. That, and being in the law offices of Skidmore, Delaney and Pfitz about fifteen years back to receive a certified check in the amount of $7,732,409.67, the final disbursement of his mother's estate, thus finalizing the probate of her will. He also inherited the family house, Eden Glade, a French Tudor affair on an oversized, gently sloping and artfully landscaped lot; somewhere in the neighborhood of nine hundred acres of canyon land in the Oklahoma panhandle; and a 1970 Ford Country Squire station wagon, white over saddle. His mother, inexplicably, had been unceasingly devoted to said vehicle, a devotion evident in the car's sparkling condition on the day of her demise.

So then, pretty much, Mr. Armbruster's life arc across maybe thirty years of more-or-less adult living, sort of, had been: man-about-town, man-about-town and political candidate, man-about-town and political washout.

Still, it's hard to ignore a man-about-town, and few in town did. And Mr. Armbruster was, if nothing else, skilled in not letting pesky facts dent positive assumptions and inferences made by his fellow townspeople, the sort of assumptions and inferences people without serious money made about people with serious money, even if they didn't know it. Actually, especially if they didn't know it.

When the front office secretary asked, in the late afternoon of April first, if Walter had found a speaker he replied simply, "Yes. Terson Armbruster."

She was without response, at first. She had never reckoned Walter as much more than the son of a one-bay mechanic, a man who had worked his way through two years of community college, then Valley State U. Who always taught the humanities wherever his assignment had been, and who had sponsored the Esperanto Club for the two years Pilkens High, somehow and for some reason, had such an organization. Who waited his turn to become a principle, as high a social standing in town as he was likely to achieve. His answer regarding the commencement speaker, quick and nonchalant and therefore honest and without affectation, had diverted her flow of thought and prevented her own quick reply, for Walter Richardson had just called man-about-town and bon vivant T. Peterson Armbruster, *Terson.* She knew Mr. Armbruster's friends called him by that casual front-chopped abbreviation, and now so did her superior, Walter Richardson – the most vanilla-est of men. A man who carried Wendy's coupons in his wallet. A man who drove a fourteen-year-old Mazda Protege with a license plate frame that stated *My Other Car is the USS Enterprise*. "You mean," she finally returned, "Peterson Armbruster? *T.* Peterson Armbruster? *The* Peterson Armbruster?"

"Yes, *the* Peterson Armbruster. How many could there be, after all." Even before finishing that answer Walter was unhappy with his response to Ms. Clark, or Wanda as her friends called her, and as he called her in his dreams. He knew his answer to her had been brusque, and in no way advanced his third-of-a-decade-long gossamer hope to have reason to call her Wanda. Specifically – as in so very, very specifically – to call her Wanda while he did her on the chemistry bench after hours and amidst the gas outlets for the Bunsen burners. *Oh Wanda, oh Wanda* he had said dozens if not hundreds of times in his dreams *I have pined for so very long to show you my DNA*. "You know, I was surprised he said yes. Um, are you?"

"Yes I am. Maybe … you could introduce me. I mean, at the commencement, anyway."

"It would be my pleasure, Wa—Ms. Clark." Terson. What kind of nickname is that? The guy couldn't have gone with Peter? He had a cousin who went by Liam in an uppity way. Walter never liked him. Still, Liam's family received a huge insurance settlement when his daddy survived, however barely, that plane crash near Topeka, which had led to a house with three bathrooms and one of those Lincolns that was really just a Taurus and circular Caribbean cruises. Liam, then. But Terson?

She aimed now to know more. After two crashup marriages – no children – she thought she was finished with men, but here was Walter Richardson, never married, not exactly young anymore. She was pretty sure he wasn't gay and she knew he made north of ninety-five K and apparently spent only about half of his post-tax income. Her good friend Naomi at People's National had told her, despite protocol, that he had more than two hundred thousand in CDs. Maybe he would clean up pretty good. Good enough, anyway. "Not too many people call Mr. Armbruster by his nickname. You know, Terson."

"Well, he asked me to. He insisted on it, actually."

"Oh really?"

"Well, yes. That's right, Ms. Cl—"

"Mr. Richardson!" Wanda interrupted. "Would … would you do me a favor? A big favor. It would mean a lot to me."

Oh God yes, Wanda, anything at all. "Well, I think so."

"Please. Call me Wanda."

"Oh. Yes. Well then, um, all right. I'd … I'd be happy to call you Wanda. Wanda." He knew neither the actual words he had just said nor their delivery had been enough, woman wooing wise. He had taken his cousin

Alberta to the senior prom, for the love of Pete. He once dated a woman for seven months, and then she disappeared and became a man. He had books, hidden in his crawl space, offering advice and ideas and step-by-step instructions on sociability. Truly, church mixers seemed to Walter to be the work of Beelzebub.

He said *Please call me Walt* at the same time she asked *May I call you Walter?* and their sentences collided and hung in the air in a heap until, thank God, the Mellilo boy wandered into the outer office.

By the final bell on that April 1st word had spread across the school about what had already been christened "the Armbruster speech." The previous anticipation of Lila Penney-Pearl had caused a predictable buzz. After all, some people in town had already seen her in *The Conniving,* which had played in theaters here and there on its way to video. But Terson caused a more rooted sort of expectation, due to the fact he was homegrown, and not particularly accessible. "Wow! What a catch, Walt," assistant football coach and world history teacher Leo Patankas said at lunch.

"I never, ever would have thought of Terson Arm-bruster, Walt," said Spanish teacher Janice White. "Good choice. Wonderful choice. Muy bueno!"

Later after lunch, though, Walter was alone in the

outer office with Skip Turner, eleven and twelve A—L counselor. "Hey, I heard about Armbruster. For this year's speaker."

"Yeah," Walter beamed, "I'm surprised he said yes. I'm looking forward to his, um, to Terson's speech." Walter found no smiling agreement in Skip's face. "Well, aren't you?"

"Oh sure. But…."

"Yeah?"

"Well, do you think there's enough meat there? Will he be able to talk to the kids about something more than spending someone else's money? The thing is, I've heard some things about Armbruster. Kind of nutty things, Walt, just between us. I guess I'm thinking of how close we came with that Kennedy kook."

Walter eyed Skip before answering. "Yours is the first negative feedback I've had all day, Skip. I think this will work out."

"I wouldn't call it negative. I'm just curious, I guess. Um, how did you contact him?"

"Well, I didn't. He contacted me actually. It was a real surprise." At that moment Walter did consider that Terson had said yes to a question that hadn't been asked.

"Oh," was the extent of Skip's reply, until "Did he mention what the theme of his speech might be?"

"Well, no. I guess he didn't, now that I think about it. But I'm sure he'll think of something. I mean, I'm sure it will be meaningful to the kids. I know they're already talking about it."

"I'm sure they are. It is exciting for them. Well, I'm looking forward to it!"

Walter went into his office, shut the door and sat down. Planting seeds of doubt in Walter had never been hard. His own mother, bedeviled by the idea of her son going away to college, had warned him of "loose girls who will drag you into the flaming pit of hell before you know what's what." His best childhood friend had accidentally and unknowingly convinced the young Walter that the communists had introduced rats into American sewer systems that would swim into American toilet bowls and bite off young American balls while said young American was doing his business and before said young American could procreate new young Americans.

Walter considered Skip a good friend, a true friend, and confided in him and valued his opinion. True, Terson had not mentioned what the content of his speech might be. Maybe Skip had a point. "How to Inherit Money," "How to Lose Royally in Local Politics" and "How to Spend (Someone Else's) Money" seemed to be the extent of Terson's repertoire. He began thinking of the Kennedy fraudster. But the astronaut's kid had, yes, been pretty good, after all. He did bring enough space shuttle models for every senior, and so that was inspiring, even if the models were only three inches long.

Still, though … hmm. And what sort of nutty things?

His intercom buzzed. "Yes. Ms. Cl—Yes … Wanda?"

"It's Terson, Walter. Um, Walt. Line two."

"Thank you … Wanda." And now the seed was obliterated. Walter punched up line two. "Hi, Terson! What's up?"

Walter heard only silence, then, "Um, who is this?"

"It's, it's Walt … ter, um, Terson. Walt. Richardson. Walter Richardson."

"Oh, yes of course. Walt. Good to hear from you. What can I do for you?"

"Well, um, Terson, heck, buddy, you called me."

"Is that right. Well I suppose I did, then. Yeah. Yes. Yep. Oh I remember now, I was hoping you might have lunch with me."

"Well certainly, Terson. What day? I think I can—"

"This day. TO-day. Now."

"Now? Well, um, Terson, it's already 2:30. And, well, I'm afraid I've eaten lunch. I ate at, well, you know … at lunchtime, I'm afraid."

"I see. I see I see I see. Well how about that. Eating lunch at lunchtime. I can understand that. I can indeed. Well, now. Well, now. Well now how about dinner then. Eight o'clock? At my club?"

"Yes. Certainly. Of course. I'd be delighted! Terson."

"Good, then. See you then. Walt. Right?"

Walter began to affirm as Terson clicked off.

Walter held the receiver for a moment before placing it in the cradle, kind of like an evaporating souvenir. Then he sprang from his chair and ran to Wanda's desk. "He invited me to dinner, Wanda. At his club!"

"Nice goin', cowboy. I kind of figured that's what was happening. Just one thing, though, which club?"

"Huh?"

"Which club, Walt? There are two, you know."

"I, I don't know which one. I don't know!"

"Relax. It has to be Woodmont."

"It does?"

"Sure. Figure it out. Greenwood accepts paying members of the public for a day of golf. They can just waltz right on in if they've got the dough. Meanwhile, the initiation fee at Woodmount is thirty grand."

"Yes. Of course. You're right. You're right! Thank you, Wanda." Walter turned for his office as he muttered something about thirty thousand dollars, then, with one hand holding the fist of the other, turned back to Wanda, "What should—"

"Blue blazer, gray slacks, ecru shirt – that's off white – and that tartan tie you have."

"Tartan?"

"Plaid."

"Oh, right. Thanks."

"Sure thing." As he walked back she noticed his socks

were dark ecru.

He had never been to a country club, but he figured they were nothing at all like the VFW hall, or even, probably, like the banquet room out at the Mariott. Wanda buzzed him again. "Yes?"

"Make sure you wear dark socks. Dark blue or black."

"Oh," Walter replied, pulling up a pants leg and looking down. "Right."

The men's store in town, Albertson's, was where she might have hoped Walter would go, should he need to. She knew he would need to, just as she knew he wouldn't dare go to Albertson's. "Penny's is on your way home. OK?"

"Yes. Right. Got it. OK. Thank you, Wanda."

"Sure thing. And listen," she continued, knowing he'd never eaten dinner at eight o'clock in his life, "you'll need a snack to hold you 'til eight." Then she imagined him driving into the Woodmont Country Club in a Mazda that had *19* as the beginning of its model year, but that detail would have to wait.

There was no shortage of parking spaces at the Woodmont Country Club. At first Walter selected a spot far from the entrance, but then he realized he had parked among the employee's cars. He drove to a gaggle of

BMWs and Mercedes and Range Rovers. He was a proper and legitimate guest, after all. And, besides, his decision allowed him to spot Terson's well-known silver-over-red XK8, thus confirming Woodmont as the place he should be. He still hadn't been overly sure as he had pulled into the lot, wondering how, and why, Wanda would know details about local country clubs.

Sidney Lamont had worked at Woodmont for thirty-two years as an all-around go-to guy. As soon as Walter walked through the entrance Sidney spotted him as an interloper and knew just who he was. "Are you here to meet Mr. Armbruster, sir?" There was no derision in Sidney's voice, not at all, for Sidney hated every member of Woodmont and the sniveling, pool-farting, screwing-in-the-caddy-shack spawn those members produced. He welcomed with delight any intruder – even a wallflower like Walter – who might put a bee in some member's bonnet. Who might piss in the well or secretly date the admissions officer's young teenage daughter or take a crap on the periwinkles at midnight, 'cause his shit *does* smell. In general metaphor, who might be a banana peel on the parquet corridors of Woodmont. *Lordy*, Sidney often thought to himself, *this has got to be as white as white people can get. GOT to be.*

"Um, yes, yes I am meeting Mr. Armbruster. Terson. Armbruster. Yes. I'm, I'm … Walter Richardson."

"Yes, sir, Mr. Richardson. Step this way, please."

Walter figured this man was taking him to the dining room but they ended up in an alcove on the way to the main floor restrooms. "May I give you some advice, Mr. Richardson?"

"Yes! Could you?"

"My pleasure, sir. Now just relax. Order the strip steak with Hollandaise and the special club salad. Eat slowly. You've come here to socialize. Eating is secondary. This is not the Waffle House, if you see what I mean."

"Yes. Of course."

"Around 9:30, no later than 9:45, begin to make your exit. Look for an opening if things come to that. Do not let him invite you back to his house after dinner, should he bring that possibility up. In general, go to his house only in daylight. And even then stick to the first floor."

"What?"

"I'm telling you, sir. I know what I'm talking about. Now the main dining room is at the top of the stairs, on the right. Good luck."

"Thank you but—"

"May I suggest you make your way, sir? The time is eight o'clock."

Walter looked at his watch. The time indeed was eight, and he did not want to be even a minute late, and his fourteen Wheat Thins and a banana and some orange juice had worn off.

As he walked into the dining room searching for Terson's face a hostess approached him. "Are you Mr. Richardson?"

"Yes. Yes I am."

"This way, please." She showed him to a vacant table set for two. "Mr. Armbruster will be along shortly."

A waiter came to take his drink order. "I'll have tea. Iced tea," he told the waiter. "I drove myself here. So, that means I'm driving back. Back home. Myself. So I'll have the tea, then."

"Very good, sir."

After Walter's second refill Terson strolled from the bar at 8:20, an old fashioned in one hand, the hostess in the other. "Well now, Walterson Richards – hell, son, I'd know you anywhere. Whatcha drinkin', tea? Tea. *Tea?*"

"Well, I have to drive home, um, Terson."

"Well I guess so. I guess so, I get it. I get it. Thanks for comin' on in, uh, Walterson. Randolph, bring my guest a menu, if you please."

As Walter ate his steak – so delicious he wished he could order another – and as he looked around at the wainscoting and the baronial fireplace and the sconces with the little tiny silk lampshades, the evening's talk barely qualified as a conversation. Terson spewed ninety-five percent of the words spoken, such as: "I'm thinkin' 'bout writin' a book that proves Jesus was a Viking and that he walked the lands of North America before Columbus." And, "I know you don't believe that moon landing ever happened, 'cause you're an educated man." And, "Did you know the words and music from the themes to *The Flintstones* and *The Jetsons* are completely interchangeable? Try it. I find that fascinating." And then, "I drink a pint of white vinegar every day at 9:33 a.m. Have you ever tried magnetic underwear?" And finally, "Do you think buffalo go *moo*?"

As Terson was finishing his second peach pie with chocolate sauce a lull was presented. "By the way, Terson," Walter began, "have you given any thought to the commencement speech?"

"Huh?"

"The speech. The speech for the commencement. In June? I'm, well I'm just curious, really. Have you picked a topic?"

"Oh yes. Yes, yes, yes. The speech. Well now, you see, well now the way these things seem to work, it seems to me, is to wait for the topic to pick you. See what I mean?"

"Well I—"

"Good. I'll be in touch. I do appreciate your comin' on in now."

"Oh, well thank you so much for the invitation. It was so—"

"You bet. Any time. G'night now, Dick."

Walter watched Terson return to the bar. He looked around the dining room, empty but for an elderly couple, with a combined age pushing two hundred, haunting the place. As his eyes scanned over to the hostess they caught hers for a split second before she jerked her head away. Walter walked down the staircase and out to his car, but not before he responded to Sidney's *psst*, finding a thumbs up and a happy smile.

Oh yes, it's hard to ignore a man about town, and few in town did.

The county school board seemed to have one goal over all others. That goal wasn't academics, of course, but then it also wasn't football. No, the board's enforcement of its no fraternization policy apparently took precedence over all else. Board members had once transferred a janitor to another school when they found he was working with his second cousin, Wanda had heard. Indeed, the board had successfully used psychology and myth to create a thin blue line regarding this policy.

Wanda, of course, first proposed getting together, but only after well more than one month of Walter calling her Wanda and of she calling him Walt and of chitchat beyond school business. This banter had progressed glacially; from Wanda's angle, anyway.

After serious consideration she offered the guise of a

Saturday afternoon meeting to discuss ways and ideas of increasing front office productivity. "It would be school business, Walt. That's all. It wouldn't be fraternization." She was prepared to counter his certain reticence, then was surprised when she didn't need to, unaware of Walt's dreams and daydreams of the chemistry bench.

A plus in her plan was found in the closure of all school offices on weekends. The board did not want employees, under the guise of extra work, lollygagging away weekends while using school electricity or heat, or for that matter flushing school toilets. Wanda drove to Walt's house that next Saturday. She considered her perky outfit as she wondered if she should have worn clothes more office-like, but then quickly figured that affectation would have drawn too much attention in and of itself, should someone – a board minion? – be watching. She had heard this happened. Everyone had heard this happened.

The Crown Vic parked down the street from Walt's – black plastic grille, smoked windows, spotlight, hubcaps on black wheels – gave her a start. She had no way to know, of course, that Walt's neighbor Ezra Pawlicking was one of those cop wannabes and had purchased his police interceptor at auction with 242,733 miles on the clock. Ezra lived with his mama, bless her heart.

Wanda rang Walt's bell. As he opened the door she

heard some jazz riffs coming from his stereo. She had never figured Walt for any music beyond pop dreck. Had he instead been playing Donna Fargo's "I'm the Happiest Girl in the Whole U.S.A" she would not have been surprised.

Husband number two – was that one Elwood? – had been a jazz buff and she recognized Mingus. Still, she wanted to give Walt a positive first step. "Is that … Coltrane?"

"Well, no. It's Ch—, um, Mingus. But I could put on some Coltrane. Wanda."

"Oh no. This is fine."

"Well, I guess I should turn it off anyway. You know, so we can … work."

"Why not just turn it down."

"OK. I see you have a folder. Ideas? You know, for the office?"

"I do. They're self-explanatory. I'll just leave them on your coffee table. Listen, I was thinking. Would you be inter— I mean, well, how about lunch. Somewhere. Not here, of course. I mean, not in town."

"Lunch?"

"Sure. I thought maybe over in Linville." She again expected his objection, and so came with a plan of some clandestine to ease his fears. "Here's the plan. I'll leave here in five minutes. I'll take route 22 to Linville. You leave seven minutes after I do and take route 9. We'll meet at Lulu's Café. It's on Madison, across from the library."

"What kind of car do you have?"

"What?"

"Your car. What make is it?"

"It's a Honda Prelude."

"Let's just take your car, why not."

"But someone might—"

"Today, let's just not worry about that. We're working, that's all. I'll take your file with us. See?"

Walt was already cleaning up pretty good, it seemed to her right then. His unexpected choice of music had increased her attraction to him right then and there. They walked to her car as Wanda asked, "Would you like to drive?"

Walter looked into the car. "I can't drive a stick."

"Would you like to learn?"

"Yes I would. But not today."

Moving along route 22 Wanda asked, "You know, you never told me about your dinner at Woodmont. I didn't ask, I guess, because I wasn't sure how it went. So, how did it go?" She had wanted to know all along, of course, but held open the possibility the evening had crashed and burned and that Walter had kept silent in embarrassment.

"Oh, it was very nice. The food was excellent. They served this steak that had a sort of crust on it, and yet the inside was juicy and just barely pink. It came with this sauce, Holland-something, but I didn't use it. According to Terson, the butter was from Ireland. Ireland! It was interesting, seeing how the other half live, you know. I mean, Irish butter! Kind of made me feel…."

"Important?"

"No, more like … not invisible. But then, maybe that's the same thing."

"Yeah. Maybe it is." Jesus, what a difference a slice of visibility had made in little ol' Walt. She wondered what was beneath this particular Clark Kent. What had he really dreamed of at five and then twelve and then twenty? She sure did figure at that moment his gossamer hopes hadn't been high school principal.

Astronaut.

Rock star.

Talk show host?

In the silence found in the next few miles she wondered what she could do with the house. If a production company wanted to video a family story from 1977 nothing would need to be changed in Walt's house.

Shag.

Harvest gold.

A hide-a-bed couch covered in plaid Herculon.

He had inherited the place from his parents, of

course. Wanda wondered if he slept in his boyhood bedroom. Cowboys, sailors, tame porno on the top closet shelf. She was pretty sure he didn't. But then, what if he did?

At Lulu's the hostess directed them to a table in a bay window. Not wanting to be two mannequins eating lunch, Walter suggested a table in a rear corner.

To the consternation of each, the meal stumbled along, gaining little traction. Each tried sparking conversation, but the words would fly for three or four sentences then thud and fizzle away. She asked him what the upfront initial in Terson's name stood for, and he had to reply he did not know. (Nor would he ever. Asking this question of Terson struck Walter as unseemly. As these sorts of things go, Terson's first name was Tennerson, and so the whole enchilada of his name sounded like a law firm.)

He asked her how many miles per gallon the Prelude gave. She did not have a clue. Had he watched *Saturday Night Live* last weekend? No, he had not. Did she know the reservoir was low, low enough to have city engineers concerned? Nope. Had he ever been to Kansas City? Yes, he had.

No, wait, that was Omaha.

"You know," Wanda continued as nonchalantly as

could be, "I can't help feeling we're having lunch with that eight hundred pound gorilla."

"Eight hundred—Oh! Right. Yes. I get it."

Tick.

Tock.

The waitress rescued things a bit by bringing Walter's dessert. Walter's first bite of Lulu's signature chocolate cake pushed him into, "Good God, that's delicious, so delicious. Won't you have a piece?"

"No, thanks. That much caffeine gives me a headache."

"That's too bad. Have you ever thought about the word *delicious,* Wanda?"

"Well, not specifically, no."

"It comes from the Latin *to allure.*" He turned his head to ensure they were alone enough, then leaned in towards Wanda. "I, I find you alluring, Wanda, so very, very alluring." He looked around again, then, "Wanda, I want you. I have wanted you for three years, since your first day behind your desk. And, well, I have no idea if I should have said that to you, you know, just now, but now I have said it. I've said it." He stopped himself from saying *Maybe that's your eight hundred pound gorilla.* Or from mentioning the chemistry bench.

"Yes," was Wanda's full reply, but it was a reply carried into her eyes and across her face and in the tenor of her voice.

The next morning *The Clarion* ran a short article on the first page of section B with the headline *Local Magnate T. Peterson Armbruster to Address Anthony High Senior Class.* Wanda read the article, then reread this paragraph seven times:

> Anthony High principal Walter M. Richardson has arranged for Mr. Armbruster's speech, which will be delivered at the commencement proceedings on June fourth. "We've had some interesting speakers over the years," Richardson said. "But I'm sure Terson will be a real standout."

Wanda knew, yes, she would need to be the one to move things along, which she had, but even still she had not expected Walter's reticence to still now be a partner. He seemed to quiver as the two sat on a queen bed in room 210 at the River Run Inn in Linville. "Walt, let me ask you something. And I don't care what the answer is. I really don't. Is this, well, is this your…." she trailed off, now finding her own reluctance in the asking. She was so hoping he wouldn't answer *Me? Come on! Heck no!*

"No," he told her. The directness and simplicity of his answer reassured her, and it was in fact the truth.

By the time Walter graduated from Valley State, Alberta, whose daddy had died when she was nine, had a stepsister. Susan was sweet on Walter, but Walter was too obtuse (to be diplomatic) to have ever known. Susan eventually felt so bad for the klutz that one day she lured

Walter over on an afternoon when she knew the others were at least an hour away, on the pretext of helping her with her geometry.

Susan, a hefty girl, was wearing a skirt but no panties. With Walter in her room she pulled his pants and underwear down off his skinny butt in a single motion, pushed him onto her bed and, straddling his loins, lowered herself atop him. Walter, having been in full launch mode as soon as his business saw daylight, at first protested mightily. But soon enough *NO NO NO NO* was replaced with *OH MY GOD OH MY GOD OH MY GOD, SUSAN, OH MY FREAKIN' GOD YES!* Walter being Walter, his ecstasy in flesh was in a flash replaced by nearly insane guilt, which caused Susan to spend the next forty-five minutes explaining to him that what just happened was not incest, that they were not blood related. All in all, though, the afternoon would eventually become a memory Walter cherished daily. After all, since that day he could legitimately claim his place among the initiated.

But his *no* came mostly from his seven months with Allise (now Allan), a time which, to Walter, anyway, had seemed fulfilling. Since Allise, though, times of intimacy had been few, if the meaning of few is stretched to nonsense and if multiplication by zero can be defined to yield something – anything – greater than zip.

Still, the act is pretty much like riding a bike, after

all. Just don't think about it, he told himself, just don't think about it and just don't think about just not thinking about it. And so the ending of their encounter allowed them both to forget his wobbly beginning, and Walter left Wanda with a grin and a glow.

About one week later Terson called Walter at home. "Been thinkin' about that speech, Walterson. Been kickin' around two titles – *What Can I Do to Save the World?* and *If You Want Someone to Help You, Just Look in the Mirror.* Huh? Yeah? That the deal?"

"Well, Terson, you can talk about any topic as long as you leave the students inspired, and with confidence in their futures. We've had many topics over the years."

"Like mine?"

"Well, I'm not sure about that. But it sounds like your ideas could develop into just what we need."

"Develop, huh?"

"That's right."

"Uh-huh. Well, now, about how long do these speeches go on?"

"Oh, usually about twenty minutes or so."

"But some have been longer?"

"A few. Twenty-five, thirty minutes. Thirty was the longest. But it was very good."

"Good, huh? Yeah. I see. I see. But now, some have

been shorter?"

"Some, yes."

"How much shorter? A lot?"

"Not an awful lot. I'd say one or two were fifteen minutes. That would be the minimum. Depending on the style of delivery, something like 3000 words will run twenty minutes."

"That's a lot of words. I mean…. But, heck, not for a Princeton man!"

"Oh? You're a Princeton graduate?"

"Sure thing. So was my daddy and his daddy and *his* daddy. Day sub, um," Terson continued, trying to recall, haphazardly and somewhat drunkenly, the school's motto in Latin, to wit *Dei sub numine viget.* "Anyway, listen up now, Walterson. You have free time in the summer, right? I thought I could take you deep sea fishing in the Gulf. Maybe in late June."

"Really?"

"Certainly. I'd like to show you a good time, buddy."

"That, that would be marvelous, Terson!" Walter replied, wondering if he had actually just used the word *marvelous.* For a brief moment he dared to wonder if he could, in some Cinderella sort of way, become a man-about-town. If so, he knew he would need a new car. And plaid, er, tartan underwear.

Graduation day was without a cloud. The sky existed in just two parts – the electric blue that was its color, and the sun that seemed to be the very lighting of knowledge that day. A weather front from the north crowned the day as perfect, more than Walter had ever dared hope for in his anticipation of the commencement speech zenith. To the town, or to anyone in the gym this afternoon, at any rate, *Walter Richardson*, *Terson Armbruster* and *electrifying commencement address* were all but synonymous.

The gym was packed, as never been packed before for these occasions. The exterior doors were open to admit the glorious day and Walter noticed people gathering at them behind rope barricades, the gym proper having reached its legal capacity. When he first glanced maybe they were three deep, but then only a few minutes later he saw they were five or seven deep.

A buzz of anticipation lived in the air of the place. Walter was now seated on the front row, Wanda beside him. On his other side was an empty folding chair that would be occupied by Superintendent Miller once the Superintendent introduced Terson. Walter noticed Ralph Baker, the political reporter from the *Clarion,* was among the crowd. A camera crew from KUXM was set up on a platform just in front of the bleachers. Walter had been interviewed by Chase Palmer, the editor of *Cat Call,* the school paper, about what he thought Mr.

Armbruster's words would mean not only to the class of 2012, but to the school and indeed the community.

Well now, the Superintendent had never before attended a commencement speech at Anthony High. The media had never before covered inspiring words to Anthony High seniors. Walter, heretofore, had figured Chase acknowledged him only for the purposes of mocking him.

Although Walter had gone to bed the night before as usual – 10:45 – he slept sporadically. He again relived his dinner at Woodmont, and wondered if Wanda could help him select sporting clothes for deep-sea fishing. He stared at the ceiling, wondering what the cost of mounting a sailfish might be these days. He had gotten used to Terson as a name, now finding it endearing. He knew he could never have gone by his middle name. Marv? Vin? No. Just … no.

Superintendent Miller now walked across the stage to the lectern. He called for silence and it came quickly, remarkably quickly, for everyone there wanted to be bathed in the ionized words of T. Peterson Armbruster without delay. Surely just being in the presence of this man – who lived in that fine house with those two staircases and a library and a swimming pool and a three-car garage, who drove a silver-over-red XK8 he parked in that garage next to that now dusty Country Squire, who received the Tiffany's catalogue, who had rented a cottage on the Aegean – would somehow messiah-like, by some unknown alchemy, perhaps, perhaps by some sort of sub-nucleonic particle they would intercept, put them on a happy path to carefree living.

"Like all of you," the Superintendent began, "I have looked forward to this day eagerly. But perhaps not as eagerly as you seniors, whom I'm sure appreciate how special this day will be to you as you leave these halls and go forward into larger lives. I remember being a senior, believe it or not, remember sitting as you are sitting – with my classmates, the future ahead, thinking I knew it all.

"Well, seniors," the superintendent continued with a chuckle, "I'm here to tell you what you learn after you know everything is what really counts. So let that learning begin now, with words of wisdom from our special, our very special, guest. Without further delay, please join me in welcoming T. Peterson Armbruster!"

Terson walked from stage left up to Superintendent Miller. The crowd sprang up – if indeed not launched – from the folding chairs with a thunder of applause and a roar of approval. The two men shook hands and exchanged a word or two, mouths close to ears. Terson smiled and waved both hands Nixon-style as the adoration continued for a solid half minute. Then Terson motioned everyone down and they obeyed willingly and happily and, it must be said, stupidly. The silence Terson pulled from the crowd continued, and then continued to continue. For the love of sweet Jesus, how mighty must be the currency of the words this man will soon speak that they require this silent overture? Under her purse Wanda took Walter's hand and squeezed it. The Superintendent patted Walter on the shoulder and smiled at him as he took his seat. Still, though, a silence pocked only with a cough and a throat clear and a folding-chair leg tipped with a rubber cap skipping flatulently over the gym floor filled the space.

And then finally, causing an almost orgasmic release across and among the enthralled, Terson began his address. "Plop, plop," he said. "Fizz, fizz. Oh … what a relief it is. Adios, amigos." T. Peterson Armbruster then turned and walked back to stage left.

Walter knew the key to public speaking was to first get a laugh from the audience. The ease that would follow would be as a symbolic, familiarizing handshake between the speaker and all before him. Walter allowed himself to think Terson was on the cutting edge here, that when he returned to the stage the perplexed audience would understand his ploy and be still more receptive to his message, although higher receptivity barely seemed possible.

T. Peterson Armbruster, however, did not return. And if laughter was in the audience, it was only nervous. "What is the meaning of this, Richardson?" the Superintendent demanded, and in that same moment Wanda's hand, to the surprise of them both, slipped from Walter's.

Malibu Christmas

Both Bradley and Elaine liked the last half or so of fall. Heavy, wide clouds often blocked the sun for days. Wind gusts scratched branches of the sugar maple against the clapboards. Darkness came well before six. Cold weather, in earnest, was a month off, but the dampness and wind could make forty degrees feel twenty. These details made shelter, however meager or worn, alluring. Bradley especially enjoyed his time between arriving home from school and his parents doing the same from their jobs. Sometimes he built fires from fallen branches he collected, and would read before the hearth.

Their house was once grand, or spacious, anyway, and, yes, grand enough. The neighborhood appealed to the carriage trade when the first houses were built in the early 1890s. The place had plaster walls with horsehair as a binder, and fourteen-foot ceilings. A third floor with a turret, and a back staircase. A slate roof and copper guttering. A front door with beveled panes and a coal chute in the side of the stone foundation.

When Bradley and Elaine's parents bought the place

a decade back it needed a great deal of work. Ten years on far more work was needed, tens of thousands of dollars of materials and labor. To their house, and for their house, the parents had done not much more than plug leaks and keep metaphorical bilge pumps going. There was no air conditioning, of course, except for the window unit in their parents' bedroom. The heating system was inadequate, but still cost a fortune to run. The wiring was frayed and the roof leaked.

When the family moved in Bradley was two, Elaine almost seven. Bradley had no memory of any other home, of course. Elaine told about where they lived before, in a cottage on an acre with apple trees and a small horse barn on a distant side of town. She kept secret photos of the place, given to her by Aunt Gwendolyn, which she showed to her brother, sometimes. Bradley dreamed of the place, still. He would often stare at the photos after pleading with Elaine to fetch them from her hiding place. She required him to sit in his room with the door closed while she fetched, for she was compelled to remain in control. He knew his sister's hiding place was under loose floorboards in her closet, but he respected this privacy because, as much as Elaine, he did not want to betray Aunt Gwendolyn's kindness. The parents were embarrassed by once having lived in such an errant zip code, among those who knew how to work, folks for whom the reality of daily toil was unquestioned. Both all but denied they ever had and would have been mortified by this photographic evidence. Aunt Gwendolyn knew better about children.

About two years ago Bradley asked Elaine if they could take a bus to the cottage. Did a route run out there? During the easy time after school or maybe on a Saturday? Elaine became annoyed and disappointed at the same time and turned from Bradley. Then, "Can't. It's a Sav-A-Buck now." She turned back to see a face she knew a child should not wear.

Both children wondered why their parents had had children. Them. For each the wondering was private. Neither would bother provoking a parent, and both were too polite to much burden the other.

Both the mother and the father taught at the local college, in the English department and the history department, respectively. Neither was a full professor, but those details did not prevent them from letting others assume they were, and tenured.

He drove an old Saab and she drove an old Volvo. Well, hell, of course they did. Elaine was disinterested in cars but Bradley was enamored. He disliked the Volvo, which looked like a '49 Plymouth in his estimation, and he hated the Saab, which looked like a goddamn Easter egg with a buck-toothed grin. "Can't we get a Mustang?"

he asked his father honestly.

His father looked at Bradley with an expression of vague amusement and some disdain, and then added a droll chuckle. "They're so bourgeoise Bradley. I think you know that."

At times the parents wore faces that connoted two questions. Who are these small people? How did they get in? And then they'd remember. And then they'd remember further, and understand they were legally obliged to care for them.

Or, well, anyway, for both Bradley and Elaine their parents seemed to come across in this way. Often enough.

Elaine was more subdued than her brother. She was already a junior and would be out of the house at eighteen. She was almost close enough to freedom to begin counting the months and packing the bags within her imagination. Her parents assumed she would go to the college, the tuition free to children of faculty, but she was plotting another route, to a place far away that would surely offer a full scholarship. She had the grades and the extracurriculars and would get the recommendations.

Bradley, though, had never backed away from confrontation, if it was not capricious. One night at dinner

Bradley's father said, "Well, can you believe those Gemini astronauts whizzing around up there? Those fools actually think they're going to the moon. Such a stunning display of Western hegemony."

Bradley knew his sister was shooting him a look to keep his mouth shut, but he didn't look at her. "Why shouldn't people go to the moon? I think it's cool. I wish I could go."

"I see. And just what would you do when you got there, hmm Bradley?"

"I'd explore. Make a moon map. I read that from the moon Earth would be like a blue marble, that you could block it out by holding your thumb outstretched from your face."

"And in which publication did you read this?"

"Oh, I don't know. *National Geographic* maybe."

"I know that purveyor of dominion does not come into this house."

"I guess I saw it at school. Or maybe at Scott's house."

"Scott Runyan?"

"Yes."

"Doesn't his father own that Pontiac dealership?"

"Yes, he does."

"Well, I suppose that's the sort of propaganda a man who sells domestic cars allows in his drywalled tract home."

"Mr. Runyan is a nice man," Bradley told in defense of Scott's father. "He bought Scott a model of the Gemini capsule." He also acted fatherly towards Bradley, simply because of the sort of man he was.

"Indeed. I rest my case. Any more of that bearnaise, my dear?"

"That's what I wanted for my birthday, you know. That model. It's not like I didn't say that, because I did."

"And yet what did you actually receive, hmm? And far more wisely, I'll add."

"A book."

"A *book*? *A* book? You make it sound like *The Hardy Boys*."

"Yeah. That would have been better." Indeed, few boys, if any, would likely find an interest in *The Young Person's Guide to The Crusades.*

"Bradley!" his mother finally interjected. "Your father scoured Mr. Delaney's store to find that vintage book for you."

"I'll bet he did. Sure smells like it."

"The Crusades were important, young man! A pivotal part of history."

"So, then, people can wield swords for Jesus, but going to the moon is nothing?"

"We're not talking about that. We're talking about a clash of religious convictions. Not that I expect you to—"

"*I'm* talking about *that! I'm* talking about going to

the moon. I find it interesting."

"You don't know what's interesting, Bradley. You're just…. Oh, never mind."

"Yeah, never mind. Maybe that's what you should have said when you *decided* to have me."

"Of all the insolent—You go to your room, young man."

But Bradley was ahead of this game. He had already pushed his chair back and was getting up. "On my way. You can have my dessert, Dad. Wouldn't want you to waste away."

"Bradley!" Mother again shrieked.

"And by the way, the thermometer in my room reads fifty-one degrees. Need any meat hung?"

"Bradley, you return to this table immediately!"

As he climbed the stairs Bradley declared, "And we're going to the moon. We're going to make it. It will be part of history, history teacher."

About half an hour later Bradley recognized Elaine's knock on his bedroom door. "Come in."

"You laid it on kind of heavy down there."

"So what."

"Well, Bradley, they are our parents, after all."

"Yes. A detail I can't help."

"I mean, surely you owe them some level—"

"I owe them nothing. I didn't ask to be born, or to live in a worn out old house. You always just sit there,

Elaine. Do nothing, say nothing. Well … I don't! At least I can say that." Bradley turned away. "Why can't he be like Scott's father?"

"Because he's not Scott's father. Our father is a noted historian. He's been published. He's known as an authority on medieval culture."

"Scott's father sells GTOs."

Elaine knew her precocious little brother meant more than simply expressing the cool factor of GTOs to a twelve-year-old. She knew he was really thinking *So the hell what. And welcome to the twentieth century.* "OK. Well, see you later."

As Elaine turned to leave Bradley said in earnest warning, "You know, they know about Tommy Schwartz." Elaine turned back with urgent questions in her eyes. "I heard them one afternoon. Last week. They didn't know I was in the house."

Actually, she thought, they probably did know his whereabouts. They played their children off one another in this way, even after the childish minds needed for the ploy had disappeared. But then maybe this obviousness was part of their tact, for Elaine now had a time bomb in her life.

Aunt Gwendolyn visited at least twice each year. In some years more often, but in each year mid-August and the

Christmas season were constants. She was a full decade younger than her brother. That decade fell on the calendar of years and their events in such a way that placed her in a quite different generation.

At Christmas she took them to an annual stage production of *A Christmas Carol* and around downtown to marvel at the decorations. On another day the three would have lunch at the Tulip Room in Peterson's department store before a movie at the United Artists.

When the two were younger Aunt Gwendolyn would prod her niece and nephew gently to figure out what each wanted under the tree. These days she simply asked, and this year Bradley knew he would get a four-lane Model Motoring slot car set. Even if it was bourgeoise.

And yet for both Elaine and Bradley their aunt's August visits were more looked forward to than Christmastime. That Elaine appreciated Aunt Gwendolyn's summer visits was not surprising, given her age and gender. But even Bradley anticipated eagerly this time of being shown care.

Unlike Christmas, Aunt Gwendolyn would devote a day to each child individually. On these days she would buy them school clothes for the upcoming year. She guided both children, but would not dictate. Last year Elaine was taken with the fashions coming out of London. Achieving a balance for an older teenage girl between a perceived cutting edge and Carnaby outrageousness was a challenge for Aunt Gwendolyn she was happy to not only accept but pull off. In earlier years dealing with Elaine had been easier, but dealing with Bradley's somewhat sedate tastes in clothing was always a delight.

This year Aunt Gwendolyn showed up in a red Malibu SS with bucket seats and a white convertible top. Bradley, so excited by the car, saw that his aunt clearly and deliciously didn't give one good god damn about how bourgeois her choice of cars was, or was not.

She noticed no tree in the house, not that she expected one, having provided a fir the last three years. Despite the indifference to the season the parents wafted, they had demands regarding any tree thrust upon them. They required proportion, that it fit the scale of the house. And so Aunt Gwendolyn could not simply have a nice seven-footer tied to her trunk lid. She had to pay twenty-five dollars for a twelve-foot tree, and further pay for delivery and setup, another ten dollars, all of which she considered reasonable enough, but still. That night Aunt Gwendolyn and Bradley and Elaine hauled up boxes of ornaments from the cellar. She borrowed a step ladder from a neighbor and the three trimmed the tree. Bradley spied his father beyond the banister in a dark part of the upstairs hall. "Hey Dad, what do you think? Nice, right?"

"Oh, ah, yes. It's so … seasonal."

"We're *so* glad you like it," Aunt Gwendolyn began. "Your approval is an ornament in itself!" Elaine knew, or hoped she knew, her aunt was really saying *Go to hell, jerk.*

The following afternoon the three attended the four o'clock matinee of *A Christmas Carol.* When they left the theater night was around them as a light snow fell. "They had a new Tiny Tim this year," Elaine said.

"Well, if I remember correctly from last year, Tiny Tim wasn't so tiny anymore."

"Yeah," Bradley said, "he'd packed on a few."

Although Aunt Gwendolyn did not consider pizza to be in keeping with the season, she sensed that casual hope in the children and so they walked into Antonio's.

"Well," Aunt Gwendolyn began, "this is so nice."

"Yeah. Father wouldn't hear of it."

"Oh?"

"Oh sure. He doesn't hear of a lot of stuff. Like The Beatles. Like Mustangs."

"Or, dare I say, convertible Malibus?"

"*Especially* with bucket seats," Bradley laughed. "They're so *bourgeois!*" Bradley continued laughing. "That's such a stupid word. *Bourgeois!*" he said again with royal affectation in his voice and a flit of his hand. "Do you like The Beatles, Aunt Gwen?"

"Bradley, maybe Aunt Gwen would like to discuss something else."

"No no, that's fine, Elaine. Well, Bradley, I must say I'm interested in their evolution. *Rubber Soul* is vastly different from their early work."

"Father calls it discordant," Elaine noted.

"Well, he would now, wouldn't he."

"He sure would," Bradley confirmed, "and how. And how 'bout 'Drive my Car,' you know? That tune smokes!"

"I was just thinking of that song. What do you listen to, Elaine?"

"Well, I like The Beatles. I really like 'If I Needed Someone,' you know, from *Yesterday and Today*. And I—"

"She likes Petula Clark!"

"Oh yes," Aunt Gwendolyn said, shooting a look at Bradley. "'Downtown' is a wonderful song. So well produced."

"Do you really think so, Aunt Gwen?"

"Yes. It's like, like a short story. Well, of course many songs are, but there's something spontaneous about this one."

"Yes!" Elaine agreed eagerly. "It's … it's a perfect day, the song."

"What do you mean?"

"Oh, she's always going on like that."

"Bradley!" Aunt Gwendolyn admonished again.

"Sorry."

"What do you mean, Elaine?"

"Well, you don't know a day was perfect until it's almost over. You can't plan a perfect day, they just happen. The right friend, something to do comes along, and everything falls into place, for that day. And the thing is, that the day is so ordinary, really, is what makes it special. Perfect."

"Yeah," Bradley agreed, "it's nice falling asleep with a smile on your face."

Aunt Gwendolyn did not want to spoil the evening with probing questions – not that such questions were needed, by this point in the children's lives. She knew perfect days and smiles in the dark were rare enough in the lives of her niece and nephew. She ached from the indifference her brother and his wife showed these two ordinarily perfect, perfectly ordinary children. They were everychildren. And although she thought she knew the scope of such indifference, she would soon find a fuller answer.

Bradley delighted in the sensation of being in a convertible in snow, as though this were camping on the go. He found adventure now, the windshield wipers with their quiet thwacking, the snowflakes in the headlight beams coming at them like stars might have to the astronauts in the two Gemini capsules that simultaneously orbited above not a week ago.

From the back seat of the Malibu Bradley looked at Aunt Gwendolyn's head and grinned as his eyes misted a little. That she was no child's mother seemed so disjointed to him, as if from a jigsaw life in which mismatched pieces had been forced together by a drunken, hammer-wielding assembler.

As they approached the house Bradley said, "There're no lights on." *Maybe they're not home* he thought. *Good.*

Aunt Gwendolyn, mostly to herself, said, "Hmm. That's odd." Elaine heard a small worry in her aunt's voice, turning to look at her.

They entered the house through the service door. Bradley switched on a light in the pantry and then in the kitchen. "Hello?" Aunt Gwendolyn tried. Then she nearly boomed, "HELLO? We're home. Anyone?"

The three stood silently in the fluorescent kitchen light for almost too long, then without a cue moved as a group into the dining room, and then into the entrance hall. Elaine switched on the sconces.

That no one made a sound – not a short scream or even a gasp – was as unremarkable as it was remarkable. In the middle of the entrance hall was the Christmas tree on its side, shards of broken ornaments in patterns that pointed back to impact sites. The shards reflected skewed light in ways not jolly. The two bodies, once parents, once sibling, once in-law, were not apparent immediately, although they were apparent soon enough. Certainly soon enough, but still no verbal reactions disturbed or acknowledged the scene.

The eyes of the parents, the sibling, the in-law were well open and the heads of both were attached to necks that could gain the angle they now kept only once. And then, in some sort of reaction, anyway, Elaine deflated onto her legs and into a pile and covered her face with her palms. After noticing spindles on the floor Bradley looked up. The banister along the upstairs hall now held a four-foot gap. Directly below was the human wreckage, his mother's legs perpendicularly crossed over his father's. If the tree had offered any cushion for either plummet, then it was scant and useless. Bradley began to understand what happened.

His mother, in recent years, weighed less than half of his father, for she became bony and he became fatty. Her mass could not have knocked his from complete stability, so she must have gone at him in some freak coincidence, just as he stumbled. He knocked through the wobbly banister mostly on his own, and her own momentum then carried her through the gap. She still grasped a spindle in her left hand, so maybe she tried to save herself.

None of the three, not even Aunt Gwendolyn as the adult, touched a body, or even approached the carnage pile. The present state of Elaine and Bradley's parents and of Aunt Gwendolyn's brother and sister-in-law was so conclusive that any doubt was exceeded. Any hope that might have been at least acknowledged – simply because grasping hope was what one did – had withered before they came in.

Bradley helped his sister to her feet. All three continued to observe in silence. Then the children looked at each other, and then at their aunt with nascent smiles in their eyes.

Aunt Gwendolyn remembered she had signed a document, some document, the document so many siblings sign without much thought. *Should a simultaneous event causing....*

Well, two heaped bodies on a Christmas tree was an event, alright, and apparently simultaneous in time frame in the view of the law. Across just the last minute her life path, she knew fully now, had changed in direction – changed radically – and yet she was not unwelcoming, not that she ever could have been. She glanced at her charges. They seemed to know as well.

"Aunt Gwen?"

"Yes Bradley?"

Bradley paused before continuing. "I, I would like to move from this place."

Aunt Gwendolyn turned to Elaine, catching Elaine's slight bob. Then she surveyed the entrance hall, its suggestion of Bohemian entropy and erudite living that was to, somehow in the mutual diatribe of the two, salute the common man and promote the greater good and … and…. She stared at what the two dead were wearing, at the pricey clothing and patrician footwear that often seemed to accompany ersatz earthy points of view. She wondered how the extravagances had been paid for, or if they were paid for. She again turned to look at her niece and nephew, both smiling weakly and winsomely, then walked to the table with the telephone. Outside, snow collected on the cloth top of her Malibu.

One Afternoon in the 'burbs

Over the last days of July rain fell, often heavily. A rotating disturbance over the Gulf of Mexico weakened before it could reach a hurricane metric, then moved up the Mississippi Valley and into the Ohio Valley. And so bands of blowing rain moved across that last July week and now, August 1st, continued.

This Saturday morning later became bright enough and sunny enough for long enough to dry the last night's shower from foliage and grass. The grass grew long over the past day or two, and now was on the verge of overgrown. The side taxus needed pruning even before Saturday a week and he knew neighbor Ralph looked out his kitchen door and frowned and then called wife Linda to frown with him.

Greta was twenty miles away, in Greentown, a place once independent but engulfed by suburbia half a century back. Away at a baby shower, or some such womanly diversion he was delighted to not only not be a part of, but as well delighted that the expectation he might be invited (once a possibility in the newness years of gender equality) did not emerge. "You're getting to the grass today, right?" was her goodbye. Later Ed answered the phone without looking – stupid! – and her return to his hello was, "Why aren't you outside mowing?"

Her question was fair, perhaps even good, all told, but he had no answer except for, "I'm charging the battery. Won't take long."

"Well, you know, the weather's good now. O.K.?"

"O.K."

"Yes. Well, I'll tell Valerie you said *hello*."

"Yes. Thanks. Bye." Who the hell is Valerie? Oh, the expectant mother, he guessed. Soon he was in the garage attaching the charging clips to the mower battery. Then he went online on the kitchen laptop and learned some Kardashian did something somewhere with someone. He wondered if this was the sort of news Valerie gave a crap about and then remembered his fantasy of Kardashians pulling a Thelma and Louise, but then what a waste of a classic T-Bird that would be. That mind gossamer then led, of course, to his ongoing remake of *Rosemary's Baby* in which Rosemary is not a dishrag but an Iraqi War vet who knows how to use an RPG, and after amniocentesis and an ultrasound she aborts the fetal Beelzebub, then somehow gets her hands on a surplus RPG and takes out the coven, roll credits.

He made a peanut butter sandwich with strawberry

jelly. He ate the sandwich and drank chocolate milk and felt twelve again and that was nice. Then he pulled up local radar at the same time he noticed a darkening outside and saw rain about thirty minutes out. "Oh shit."

The mower battery always charged in twenty minutes. He raised the garage door and started the mower. At least he could make several passes which would evidence his attempt to mow before rain came, but the question was where to start. He always started in the front yard – always – but figured a partially cut back yard preferable to a front yard with some kind of inverted mohawk. Now he needed a reason for later on for starting in the back yard. On the radar he had seen a solid, fat band of rain, two hundred miles north to south, moving northwest but he would, in that approaching later moment, tell her the storm was a pop up. "Yeah, heck, the darndest thing!" he would say.

After mowing a third of the way down the hill the rain opened up without overture. In seconds he was drenched and the drive wheels of the mower slipped on the wet cuttings. As he pulled into the garage his shirt clung to his skin nakedly and his hair hung over his brow like a Three Stooges stooge. The day grew even darker, which he knew indicated rain for hours. In the kitchen he confirmed this state of affairs on the radar, again, which now included color scales of approaching intensities.

He dried off and changed clothes. When did she say that thing would be over? Four, maybe? Five? If five, half an hour to drive back, maybe more because the Saturday mall traffic would be getting heavy. So … six? The present time was two forty. Three solid and unfettered hours then. Sweet!

He called other-side neighbor Danny, the good one with his own overgrown taxus, and asked if he'd like to go to lunch. Danny had eaten a late lunch at two. "Sure. I'll pick you up."

He saw Danny leave his own driveway and soon pull up to the garage. He dashed out the raised door, through the rain and climbed into Danny's '91 Beemer, an 850i. Danny hated new cars, which to him looked like bug-eyed overfilled car balloons. He would not ride in Ed's Forester. *How can you drive that four-banger rice burner?* Danny asked silently, since he already knew the answer – knew the choices made, and by whom.

At Arby's Danny told the counter person, "Two brisket sandwiches and two large fries and two large drinks. And two cherry turnovers."

"But—"

"No, Ed. Nope, you're not ordering a turkey sandwich on my watch."

"Yeah, but I need to—"

Danny raised a palm to his friend. "OK. Look," he said to the counter kid, "make his heart healthy."

"But sir, we don't offer a—Oh. Yeah! That's funny. Hey Willy!" the kid yelled back to prep. "Only half mayo on one of those." The kid looked at Danny, then yelled again to Willy, "And double on the other!"

"You know," Danny started, looking at the kid's nametag, "um, Dakota. I think you're overqualified for Arby's."

"Ain't that the truth. Sir. That'll be twenty-two ninety."

After the two pulled out of the Arby's lot and older punk in a new M4 coupe with an automatic pulled next to Danny at a stop light. The punk lowered his passenger driver window. "Wanna go?" Danny knew the punk had really – silently – asked *Want me to leave you in the dust, old man?*

First, no dust was to be had on this rainy afternoon. Second, the suburban crawl before and around them was as antithetical to the autobahn as could be. "Yeah, not today, son. I'm on my way to the bank to cash my social security check." The subtext of Danny's reply was *Have you ever even seen a clutch? It would be right next to where you ball sack used to be.* The time was three forty five.

Ed's phone rang. This time he did check the screen, which read *Greta.* His wife's name on the screen was, in no way, a surprise. "Hi, honey!"

"Are you at home? I called the land line but you didn't answer. Did you have the cantaloupe and cottage cheese I left you for lunch? It's wrapped up on the second shelf."

"Not yet. I'm in … well, where are you?"

"On my way home. I'll be there in about fifteen minutes."

"Oh. Oh? Um, how's Vicky?"

"Who?"

"Vi—Valerie."

"Oh she's fine. She received some lovely things for the baby. I'll show you the pictures."

"Oh, yes, great." He stopped himself from adding *Looking forward to it* which would have likely screwed this pooch.

"Did you get the grass cut?"

"Well, I started. But there was a pop up storm. Just … popped up! Never saw it on the radar."

"Well it sure is raining where I am. Doesn't look like a pop up to me. The skies are so dark. And—hey, you know what? I see Danny up ahead. How 'bout that?"

"Yeah. Wow!"

The dark skies were above Danny and him, of course, and determined rain continued falling. He was going to ask where she was but didn't as he remembered she would, of course, be on Greentown Road and then remembered they were presently on Greentown Road.

"Get down," Danny instructed.

"What?"

"Get down!" he repeated, putting his right hand on Ed's head and pushing down. "Wife at nine o'clock."

"Whose?'

"Yours! You know, Greta? The one you just talked to?"

"Whoops," Ed said as he slinked into the seat well.

Danny's phone rang. "Danny? This is Greta! Look over. I'm right next to you. Isn't that wild?"

"Oh, yeah, it sure is, Greta. Imagine seeing each other on Greentown Road! Wow."

"Well I just talked with Ed. I guess he's in the garage."

"Uh, yes. He's probably getting some of the wet grass off his mower. I saw him cutting earlier."

"Did he finish?"

"No, the rain came. Just all of a sudden."

"Well I knew he wouldn't finish because he didn't start this morning first thing and now, well…."

"Yeah, well, that's how it goes sometimes, Greta,"

"I guess. But he should have charged the battery yesterday. Or early this morning,"

"Oh, I agree. That would have been wise, because now, well…."

"Exactly. You know Ralph keeps such a nice yard."

"Oh, yes, Greta, you're right about that. There's

something to shoot for."

"And he goes to church with Linda. And he's a Boy Scout leader."

"Yes, well, he does look always prepared."

"Yes! Well, bye now, Danny."

"O.K. Goodbye, Greta."

Danny and Ed moved ahead twenty feet before Ed's phone rang again. A glance at the screen was not needed. "Hi, honey!

"Oh you'll never guess who I just saw."

"No?"

"No. Danny. And I think I saw him pulling out of that Arby's, you know, on Greentown? Across from the nice McDonald's?"

"Oh?"

"Yes. You know, he shouldn't eat there. So, did you eat the cantaloupe I fixed?"

A tossup. Roger covered his phone. "Can we beat her home?"

"I think so."

"Yes. Just now. Delicious. Thanks."

"Oh well you're so welcome. That Danny. I wonder what Ellen would think if she knew? Oh, well, that's none of our concern, I guess, now is it?"

"Oh, no, yeah, not at all."

"So are you in the garage? Cleaning off the mower?"

"Yes. Hard at it. Ready for tomorrow. Good day,

tomorrow. I'm sure of it."

"Well then I'll see you soon. Maybe we can OH MY! Look at that. Danny just ran a red light! I'm so glad you don't ride with him. You know people in Subarus don't run red lights."

"Oh, don't I know it. Well, see you in a bit." Then to Danny, "Let's book."

"Yeah, O.K." But their lead time was scant, maybe thirty seconds. They turned off Greentown Road on to Sunnyvale. Danny was ten houses down on the left, Ed nine. They shot down Danny's driveway. Ed hopped out, ran behind Danny's house, up the side hill and into his garage through the side door, Greta pulled in ten seconds later. Ed waved at his wife and pretended to wipe his hands on a rag. He walked quickly into the house but not too quickly, grabbed the plate of cantaloupe and cottage cheese from the second shelf of the refrigerator and ran with it into their bedroom, shoving the plate under the bed. Then into the bathroom, where he had thrown his wet clothes into a pile in a corner, just the sort of shenanigans that drove Greta nuts. He starts hanging the wet clothes over the shower rod.

"Ed?"

"Yeah, back here honey." From the bathroom he noticed the bed skirt was cupped upward where the plate had gone in. He kicked it into compliance just as Greta entered. "Hey, let's see those pictures!" he beamed even as he considered this move of conciliation might be suspiciously too soon.

"Oh, sure. Just let me sit down for a moment."

Later she wondered where his lunch plate was, of course. But then a man's work is never done.

Maybe He'll Be in for Christmas

About the time the leaves began falling Aaron started packing a lunch to eat in his truck. He had a little radio and a handheld digital TV, picked up at the Radio Shack, plus long underwear and electric socks and a little crank-powered lantern. He wasn't coming in 'til seven at the earliest now, and Mother and Father had eaten dinner precisely at six for somewhere in the neighborhood of the last 22,000 evenings. Sometimes he wasn't coming in 'til nine or nine thirty, well beyond dark. Sometimes he picked around in the refrigerator or the pantry, but if it were one of those closer-to-nine nights he'd probably already been to the Arby's a piece out or that Subway over down there. "Well," Mother noted to Father, "sitting in a truck all day doesn't burn many calories." There was a gardener's toilet in the garage, and the side garage door was out of sight from the back view of the house, so there was that taken care of.

The situation had reached a point. Now Aaron was spending all day in his truck. He still ate breakfast in the house, sometimes with both or one of his parents, although he's never been much of a breakfast eater.

His boy's slim a.m. appetite has dismayed Father considerably since Aaron was small. Father has sat down to two eggs over easy on toast, a half dozen strips of limp bacon, grits or hash browns or both, sometimes a biscuit or two, fresh juice and coffee for somewhere in the neighborhood of the last 24,000 mornings. Not infrequently he would have a cinnamon roll or a slice of butter kuchen for morning dessert. And here was his son eating like a picked chicken. What's anyone to do?

Aaron's truck was a two-decades old Chevy. It was full-sized but with a short bed and no four-wheel drive so it wasn't tall and not really imposing. Compared with present day overstuffed trucks, the Chevy was almost within spitting distance of cute. It was red. The trips to the Arby's or that Subway, and sometimes that used book and record store out the way over there, were the extent of Aaron's driving. Subtracting the present odometer reading from the reading one year earlier on this day gave a difference of 817.8. Which is to say, miles.

Brook Drive had been an upscale address for eighty years or more, and remained so. Faithful enough Tudors and too-large Cape Cods, scattered Cotswold cottages and Corinthianed colonials, once costing maybe seventeen grand, if that, when Mr. Roosevelt was still in office now sold routinely for twenty-five times as much, often more. Much more. Still, as an older neighborhood it sported a lived-in, casually overgrown look unlike the Barbie castles way out yonder with edged beds visible from space and dyed mulch and green grass in the middle of a hard January. In other words, one couldn't simply assume every resident on Brook Drive was a Republican. Whereas a red pickup that rarely moved and that now housed a little-occupied man for the better part of each day would have been a real attention getter in Perfect World, to the extent of yanking the respective chains of the neighborhood watch, city council members and wannabe cops who now really were cops along the tightly curbed expanses of, e.g., Choppinghouse Trace, Brittany Vale Court and Hamptonshire Lane ("Maybe somebody should call Homeland Security about that guy, huh?"), whereas that hoopla somewhere else, along Brook Drive Aaron was nothing less and nothing more than a facet or two of life. Children on the way home from school waved to him and he waved back. Folks walking their dogs or just themselves would stop and Aaron would roll down the window and talk with them in a happy way that encouraged return visits. At this time of year those folks would comment on the wreath he had wired to the grille. Sometimes Mrs. Worth would bring him hot cocoa and the chocolate chip cookies she made with raisins. Aaron never figured out the raisins, but he always thanked Mrs. Worth of course, and then commenced to pick out the raisins with one tool or another on his Swiss Army knife, or simply eat around them.

Sarah lived right across the street from Aaron. She watched him frequently from her upstairs bedroom window, but Aaron never caught on. At her beginning she was measured out about the same helping of gumption as Aaron, her last really big day being a journey to the movies to see a revival of *Singin' in the Rain.* That was a year and a half back. Given a market for Emily Dickinson impersonators she might have known a hot career. She made tea a lot. Read. Wrote poetry.

But then....

Christmas Eve was unseasonably warm, to the extent of having a wintertime thunderstorm unfold in the yule skies as warm air moving up the Mississippi Valley was colliding with a Canadian cold front that dipped into the weather map like a hammock with fat old Uncle Will lying in it. Thunder and lightning were unusual enough in December, but this display was really quite something.

Sarah was sitting in her bedroom … well, of course that. Where else? She was intrigued by Aaron sitting in his truck and occasionally driving it somewhere. Anywhere was enough of an appeal to Sarah to wonder just where.

On the roof peak above her side window was an old exterior TV antenna her father meant to take down since maybe around Bush 41, but he just never got to the chore, or perhaps more to the point never allowed the chore to get to him. The bottom of the antenna mast came about halfway down the side exterior wall that included Sarah's bedroom. Ionic atmospheric disturbances of positive and negative (+ - + - + - + - and so on and so forth and etcetera) approached her house and then engulfed it momentarily as they passed over and around. The old TV antenna caught a gazillion + - + - + - s which, operating over time distances for which whole seconds were without usable resolution, reached the bottom of the mast with nowhere to go but to zap (zippity zap zap **ZAP!**) across her room to find a cast iron vent pipe in the wall beside her closet door. Luckily, no wiring was in the vicinity of the pipe or the bottom of the antenna mast. The vent pipe was for the powder room off the entrance hall. The powder room sported a gold peacock-motif wallpaper, in vogue four decades back, and between the wall and the back of the toilet tank the crisped remains of a potpourri, scentless since probably around the time *Murder She Wrote* was cancelled.

"WHAT THE HELL WAS THAT?" Sarah shouted louder than she had ever shouted any words, which was almost never. The utter shock of her own reaction to herself for a few seconds shoved her mind away from the meteorological phenomenon that just invaded her room like some Star Trekkian ion beam, for she never even thought to say *HELL* or even just *hell* (in that exasperated way to suggest resignation) at any time over the last maybe 19,412 days, since about the time she learned to string a few words together into a coherent sentence.

She gasped, and flung her fingers to her open mouth, stunned by her own words and by further errant thoughts that ricocheted inside her skull like untied party balloons. These thoughts included watching something on HBO, wearing dungarees, quitting the church choir and, perhaps, subscribing to *Cosmo*. But what if Mother found the magazine in the mailbox one day? What if mother had a fainting spell wondering what the postman must think?

For quite some time she's wanted to put pecans in her chocolate chip cookies.

Aaron.

Her head hurt.

The acrid smell of singed hair, then, yanked her attention back to the reality of living on a planet with a vibrant atmosphere. She ran to a mirror to find herself sans eyebrows, and with the remainder of her bangs kinked away and nearly smoldering, or so she imagined. Her forehead looked sunburned. The entrance and exit points of the bolt left charred splotches the size of salad plates on opposite walls. For God's sake that sideways lightening had all but vivisected her from one temple to the other! "Hey! I was almost killed up here! Hey! Anybody? Jesus Christ, people, a little help?" Well, not killed, clearly. Still, her use of *almost* was far slimmer than she knew and had she seen an EEG of her brain right then and knew what she was looking at compared to the baseline from her adult life (until just very, very recently), well…. On second thought, let's be glad she didn't see her present brain quantified.

Anyway, no one came running, not just right then. Her own set of Mother and Father was at the caroling and ninety-proof nog shindig next door at the Palmers. ("Look, Muriel, I'm not staying for 'The Twelve Days of Christmas' again this year. OK? It's like a yuletide 'Ninety-Nine Bottles of Beer on the Wall,' for Pete's sake.") But then just as well they hadn't been on site, all told, really, for how could she explain her blasphemy? But by the next second, she was wondering why the hell she would ever have to explain. For the love of Pete she was a grown woman. "Man," Sarah said to herself aloud, "I should blow this joint once in a while." Her head didn't hurt so much now. She looked back in the mirror to see herself dressed in what had long ago become her de facto uniform – a knee length navy skirt of cotton gabardine, a cotton white blouse with a Peter Pan collar, her hair fastened behind her at that collar, black flats. She cocked her head like a dog and said, "How 'bout me and you breakin' on through to the other side?"

Behold, the Night of Zap. The power of Zap.

As the storm first began in earnest Aaron's mother called him on his cell and asked him to come into the house for his own safety. "For me, Aaron? Would you do this for your mother on Christmas Eve?" He obliged. He helped trim the tree convivially, even as the three watched the storm with some apprehension, and then went to bed. His parents were delighted, and relieved, really, although only in a very guarded way and so they did not assume anything was really changed, Aaron-wise. But, still, the three had a marvelous time, one amplified by being in the shelter of their home during the storm. Despite the balminess a fire was laid. And so Mr. and Mrs. had that going for them, anyway. ("It's more than some have," Mother later reassured Father. "We're lucky, tonight.")

By eight the next morning he headed for his truck,

even though the temperature was no higher than thirty, having dropped by more than half during the night. A rare hoar frost now coated the outside world. Aaron assured Mother and Father he would be back in after not too long, promising Father whatever pre-noon feast Mother whipped up he would eat and enjoy in keeping with the day. "Heck, Father, I'll eat a foot-high stack of flapjacks with butter and syrup and whipped cream and shaved chocolate. Bacon. And a big glass of egg nog. A real Christmas breakfast!"

In the truck now, beginning day 20,999. He brought along a copy of *Breakfast of Champions* to begin again, but before he opened the cover decided some general universe contemplation was more in order. Contemplation of the universe required laser-beam focus, which to the general passerby, particularly random non-residents of Brook Road, looked pretty much like catatonia. Sarah's window taps at first went unheard.

Eleven hours earlier Muriel and Edgar had rushed back next door from the Palmer's after hearing the crack boom bang, hence zap. Muriel burst through the front door and cried up the stairs, "Sarah! My goodness gracious Sarah are you all right?" Edgar, who kept an imagination of pessimism, began a visual and olfactory exploration, convinced fire – if not a downright hideous and consuming conflagration – was hiding somewhere. These things can smolder, he'd heard. For hours sometimes. (IF NOT DAYS! His imagination then suggested.) Thankfully, fire was not hiding within the walls like pesky scratching mice, for the cast iron vent pipe and the copper water pipes adjacent had provided an excellent and containing ground.

"Yes, I'm all right, Mother. Just a little…."

"A little? A little what, Sarah? A little WHAT?"

"Just a little singeing, that's all."

"Singeing? Edgar, we're taking Sarah to the hospital," Mother commanded. Her eyes teared as her voice slid into a quiver. "She's been singed!"

"Mother, I do NOT need to go to the hospital."

"I insist! I absolutely insist! You've been singed! Edgar our child has been singed! Brutally singed! Violated! Edgar? EDGAR! Do something!"

"NO Mother. N-O, no."

Stunned, Mother was gape-mouthed. "Sarah? Sarah! What has gotten into you? You're taking a tone, daughter, a tone, I tell you. I, well I mean, well … honestly!"

Returning to the entrance hall from wherever he had been Edgar informed, "There doesn't seem to be a fire, Muriel. Do you smell anything? Use your nose, woman.

Your nose!" Edgar instructed. After brief further consideration he declared, "The attic! I must check the attic!"

"But Edgar! Sarah is taking a tone! When has she *ever* taken a tone? Edgar? Edgar! Oh my goodness gracious amidst blessed creation all Hades must be breaking loose! Beelzebub and his rabble-rousers are among us, I tell you, WINGED HELLIONS AMONGST US! Edgar? EDGAR!"

The next morning Muriel and Edgar slept 'til ten despite the presence of this particular day. The party and the nog had not much to do with their Hollywood hours. They always slept 'til ten, or nine thirty, anyway. But on this day's morning Sarah became an earlier riser.

So, then, finally Aaron did hear Sarah's taps. He rolled down the driver's window halfway, against the drag of peaky frost, to see a woman dressed in the musty clothes she found in her brother's old bedroom closet. The jeans and shirt fit well enough to not be clownish. A messenger bag was over her right shoulder. She had no eyebrows and the front of her hair was partially gone in a ragged way and her forehead was red. He had a feeling he should know her. "Yes?" he answered with the vaguest demand.

"You're Aaron, aren't you. I'm Sarah. I live across the

street."

"Oh?"

"Yes. And, Merry Christmas."

"Oh, yes. Merry, um, Merry Christmas. Sarah."

"I've noticed you're out here. A lot."

"I am out here a lot. So, well, I mean … do you watch me, or something?"

"I do. It looks to me like you contemplate the universe. A lot."

"Well, I *might* do that. It's just that—"

"I do that. A lot."

"You, you do?"

"Sure. Up there." She pointed to her front bedroom window. "I've seen you. Like I said, a lot. Just watched you, really. Do you mind?"

Aaron thought intently for a moment, then answered directly and honestly, smiling and shaking his head side-to-side, "No."

"Look, um, would you mind if I got in there with you? It's kind of cold. Damp. Extra frosty."

"Um, no. Yes. I mean, I'm sorry. Yes, please get in." He started the truck for his guest. The frost had found a path to the rubber seals between the door frames and the truck body. Aaron needed a wooden stir stick for paint buckets to edge around the seal and break the hold before his door opened. Sarah pulled on the passenger door handle as Aaron pushed from inside until the door broke away from the weather stripping. A couple of seconds later she got in. "We'll have some heat in just a minute. Not too long. This truck has a good heater." He had liked sitting inside the translucence the frost gave, however cold, but found himself eager to please his visitor. Sarah didn't say anything as Aaron wished she'd say something. "Do you like music?"

"Everyone likes music. It's hardwired in our brains."

"Oh. Well, I just—"

"What do you do, all day out here in your truck? I mean, I'm just curious. Besides universe contemplation."

Aaron did not reply straight away. Then he looked at her with scrunched eyes. "Look, do you *really* contemplate the universe, up there?"

Now Sarah did not reply as a given. After a few long seconds she said, "Yes, I do."

"So, you've watched me, then."

"Yes."

"How long?"

"Long. Very long. Years, really."

"Why?"

"You're something of a variable. You're predictable in an unpredictable way."

"Oh," he said, looking straight ahead. Then he turned to her. "Would you say predictable unpredictability is to be distinguished from unpredictable predictability?"

"Of course."

"I see. Good. I understand. What do you do, then?"

"I asked you first."

"Oh. Yes, you did. Well, you know, I'm thinking we might do the same things."

"That's what I'm thinking. So, we have universe contemplation in common. But you do write?"

"Well, yes. Do you?"

"Yes. Poetry."

"Prose."

"I know."

"How."

"You don't look up enough for poetry. Prose needs less contemplation, or less while you're actually putting pen to paper, anyway. May I see yours?"

"Could I see yours?"

"Of course." She pulled out some loose sheets from the messenger bag. "Here."

He opened the glove box. His sheets were bent. "Here."

He read:

Mildred and William

Day-to-day events making world history stole the youth
     from each
but more Millie
She had waited sixteen years for this day

Bill some fraction of that number
his family largely unwrenched by Black Tuesday
The Depression, for some, having been like a skipping
      tornado
But then his unit swung open the Dachau gates
There was that multiplier – the utter depths of
      inhumanity, then
so Bill was ready, too

Millie in particular had endured sameness
going to bed wondering when
or if
a different tomorrow might come, ever or otherwise
More than five thousand mornings awakening to stasis
or change that made bad news nothing but worse

An edge made keener by enervation and raging if quiet
      desperation
the ultimately indistinguishable itches of anxiety and
      longing
For William by skeletons still alive with eyes so vacant
they let some ooze from the backside of the universe leak
      onto this plane

Things go better with Coke

A quarter-acre of Earth
Cape Cod facsimile
The rarefied luxury of routine daily life now
reading the paper
eating dinner

food, then simply buy more
new cars and gasoline
and then simply buy more
listening to the radio now
watching the radio soon

See the U.S.A in your Chevrolet

War children play on the floor
The post-war children awaiting their cues
All the children will be young enough to possess
gleefully unknowingly
youth unstolen
To not have that shadow drop across
the coming volcano of fantastic abundance

Shake it up baby, now
Twist and shout
The Eagle has landed

While she read:

There's a Brother in Your Driveway

Mark wasn't too much of a mechanic, but then Ellis was no kind of mechanic. On Saturday Mark worked on Ellis's '99 Cutlass, an Oldsmobile that was simply a thinly veiled Chevy Malibu. The odometer displayed 132429. Somehow and by some dumb luck that collection of miles had rolled into place, considering when Mark popped the hood that morning Ellis was two quarts low, and what oil did display itself on the stick was black and gritty. The air filter seemed to have been in the vicinity of an erupting volcano in the last few days, and the radiator took a full gallon of Prestone 50/50.

Mark changed the oil and filter on the driveway, turned by years and weather into asphalt gravel and weeds and puddle-holding ruts. He replaced the air filter, added the antifreeze and filled the tank with Shell regular after putting in a bottle of injector clean-er. The transmission fluid might have been worse, and, besides, Mark didn't know how to change the fluid, wasn't going to find out, and wasn't spending any more money or time – which is to say of his and no one else's, as the deal was playing out.

Mark was genuinely trying to help his brother. He was also trying to improve the odds that the loca-tion of the breakdown would be far enough away so that Mark's entire involvement – expected, implied or otherwise – could and would be only *Hey, I'm sorry to hear that*, if and when Ellis called.

Sometimes Mark reminded himself he had a brother. Ellis had left for Wisconsin, on full scholar-ship, when he was only seventeen, Mark seven. Mark had memory flashes of Ellis in the house, but no continuous memory chunks of Ellis in daily living.

About once in each year, usually during the first days of fall arriving for certain, Mark would take down an album from the top shelf of the coat closet. The cover of the album showed a New England harbor scene, which always struck Mark as dis-jointed and slightly absurd. Inside were the photos of himself as a very small child with his parents and his sister, and Ellis. Clearly Ellis was his brother. Still, as Mark saw it Ellis had gone off to Madison, and never came back. Christmases and Summers? Maybe, maybe not, or so memory seemed.

"Thanks for working on the car. How did you learn to do that?"

"Like anyone else. I figured it out. That's like asking how did you learn to wash dishes."

"Well, I guess you have a point. You know, when I left after Mom's funeral, I felt awful. About everything, of course, but also about you. Particularly about you. That I was leaving you to…."

"To what?"

"To this," Ellis said, waving his hand to indicate the house and every doodad and worn piece of furniture in it. Everything in it, including Mark. Mark had inherited the house neither sibling much wanted anyway.

"Maybe it's what I want. What's wrong with—"

"No it isn't."

"You don't know that. What's wrong with my life?"

"Yeah. Nothing."

"Screw you."

"Yep, there's nothing wrong with croaking where you grew up. In the same room, in the same bed. You do know your slot car set is on the top shelf of that upstairs hall closet, don't you? In its original box."

"I have a good job."

"A tech writer for a startup? Mark, you're fifty years old. Unmarried. Ungirl-friended. Just … un."

"Yes. And not divorced three times. And not sixty. And not never tenured anywhere. Even Nowhere College wouldn't give you tenure. And now you limp into the driveway of a brother you've never really known to regroup. All but broke. I know why you're in town – because you think you can get some cash out of Sally. Sadly, you probably can."

Ellis looked away before answering, "You know nothing of academic politics."

"No. I don't. Your car is ready to go. You can leave in the morning."

On Friday night Mark heard Ellis creeping around the house after they both had gone to bed. He knew Ellis was looking for the cash and the silver bullion their dad once stashed in various locations within the house, behind false walls and dummy joists. Mark let him look, taking some pleasure in the rustling sounds, he admitted to himself. All his hidden treasure was needed after Dad died.

That Ellis didn't know that about their mother's situation, or wouldn't bother to figure it out, irked Mark. Both Ellis and their sister agreed the house should be Mark's, who had given ninety-five percent of the effort and time needed to keep their parents out of nursing homes. Besides, Ellis figured the place needed fifty thousand in updates.

Ellis did not leave Sunday morning, or at any time along Sunday. Mark didn't need to be at work until eleven Monday morning. He wanted Ellis long gone before he left for work. He had refused to give Ellis a key, and now he knew a confrontation was

Aaron read Sarah's poem two times, then waited patiently and silently for her to finish his story. Then she said, "This is much better than I expected. What I mean is…. Look, I like it. I really do. It reminds me some of Updike."

"Or Cheever, maybe."

"Yes! Do you like Waugh?"

"Enough."

"Exactly. Me too. So, I guess your mom must have called you, since you stopped in mid sentence."

"Yep."

"Yeah, I know how that goes. Chasing an idea, and somebody wants to know where the tea strainer is."

"Or the spray starch," he chuckled. "Your work is fantastic. It really is. I like your injection of commercialism as juxtaposition, the underlying commodification. May I read others?"

"Of course. May I?"

"Certainly."

Save for the heater blower, silence for a bit. Then, "I'd like to tell you something."

"Oh?"

"I think I was struck by lightning last night."

"Really?"

"I think so. Almost, anyway. Very close."

"Oh! That boom last night. The flash! And your eyebrows. And the hair! Your skin! Are you OK?"

"Yes I'm OK. But … I think might be a little different now. Maybe. But I think that's OK."

"Hmm. Do you think the experience will change your abilities?" He raised her typewritten sheets and waved them.

"I don't think so. Wait. Yes, I hope so. Hell, maybe I should have been struck by lightning a long time ago."

"I think I know what you mean. I mean, in the larger sense. The largest sense."

"Really?"

"Sure. Well, I think so, anyway. It's, it's like being a Ferrari, but there's no gasoline."

She did not reply, but a wry smile grew on her lips as her eyelids narrowed a bit and sparks bounced from her green irises. Then she looked at him with appreciation and thanks and gave a slight, tiny laugh. "Yes, it is." She took a few moments to universe contemplate, then turned to look at him directly. "Look, I thought maybe we could be friends. Maybe even more than friends. Possibly. I mean if you…."

"You mean … boyfr—" Aaron gulped. "Boyfriend? Girlfriend?"

"Well, yeah. But, look, I'm not sure there'd really be any of … that."

"That's OK. I don't really have a lot of *that* experience."

"Fuel-less Ferraris rarely do. Well, I would guess, anyway."

"No. So, just wondering … how fuel-less are you?"

She paused, but only briefly and poetically. "The needle's below empty."

"Yeah?"

"Yep."

"That's nice. Maybe one day we'll get some fuel. I mean, maybe. Only if we both wanted to."

"That could happen," Sarah said, continuing her intense gaze. Then she took Aaron's hand in hers. "That would be nice."

"You know what?" Aaron asked, having pulled his hand away just a millimeter before accepting Sarah' unforeseen advance.

"What?"

"Maybe people should be struck by lightning more often."

Meeting Mr. Quinn

Ben came home for Christmas, maybe because he didn't come to his father's funeral six months earlier. Not that his appearance now was for his mother, long dead. Or for his siblings, long scattered, none returning since after the funeral to deal with the twelve-room Tudor in which they had been raised. Or the Range Rover and the two T-Birds – '56, '65 – Dad had in the garage. Or the catalogue of finery within the house. The Lehmans were once an extended family, until the extensions broke away. Broke free, maybe.

He just figured maybe he'd have a few people over, that's all. Maybe right after Christmas, before New Years. So he'd need a tree. A real one. Two carloads of women from a place called Speedy Maids gave the place a once over.

Mark hadn't seen Ben in probably twenty years. From time to time recently he drove by the Lehmans' forlorn house, for no other purpose than to remember old times for a minute or two. The place was always dark at night now, unless a raccoon tripped the motion sensor on a security light, so on this night when Mark saw the living room and the upstairs hall lit, the house caught his attention. When he saw the primo '89 Carrera, he knew Ben was home. Or in the house, anyway.

Mark circled around the meandering block in his Subaru, then circled again before deciding to pull into Ben's, stopping behind the Porsche. This despite the late hour.

Twenty years. Ben now looked pretty much like Ben then plus twenty. Enough, anyway. The door opened. "Ben? It's Mark Harris. I hope you don't mind, I know it's late. I saw the lights on, for the first time in months. Saw the car. Figured it was you. I'm afraid it's been a while. Not since Harry Doyle's wedding."

"Mark Harris. Hmm. Wait, wait, Linda Harris's brother?"

"Yeah, that's one way to put it."

"Well come on in! Sure! Are you still living around here?"

"Yep. Actually, I bought my parents' house when I came back from Dallas."

"Really?" Ben said looking around his old house. "Well, I just don't think I'd want to croak here. You know, where I grew up. But that's just me."

"I kind of thought the same, but when my mom died

I took the opportunity to buy out my sister and brother. I've always loved the house."

"What were you doing in Dallas?"

"I was in international banking down there. Got an offer from Skip Tilden one day, just out of the blue, and took it. Came back here."

"I remember Skip. He's with Latitude Funds, here in town, isn't he?"

"He was. He died a few years ago. His sailboat went down off the coast of New Zealand."

"Wow. No body, I guess."

What a strange question. "Actually, no."

"Well, forgive me, but the reason I ask is because my second wife was lost in similar circumstances. You don't really think about the importance of a body until there isn't one, you know? It's all any of us really own, when you think about it, and for survivors to be unable to deal with that possession properly, well, it's a wound that never really heals. So, anyway, aren't I off to a cheery start."

"I'm sorry to hear that, about your wife."

"I married once more. I'm finished. Never again. I'm guessing you've been married for, let's see, twenty years?"

"Twenty-one. I have 2.5 kids."

"That was my next guess."

"So, what are you doing these days?"

"Well, Mark, I've made lucky decisions. In 2005 I

put the money up for something called PlexiPlex. Twenty-somethings that looked like they were twelve were the brains behind my money, and behind my thirty percent stake. Next thing I know we've sold it to Microsoft for seven hundred thirty-two million. So what I do is what I want, which is too often not much."

"Oh. Well, I'm afraid I have to be in my office tomorrow at nine. And I drive a Subaru. Nice 911. A classic."

"Yeah, I like to keep them going. It's fun."

"Well, Ben, I, I guess I really just wanted to say hello. Like I said, it's been a long time."

"Hey, you bet! Listen, I'm having some people over, between Christmas and New Years. I'd like for you and your wife to come. I'll have to let you know. Short notice, I'm afraid."

"Well, sure! I don't think we have much planned. I'll need to ask Maria, but I think I can say yes. And, so … well, like I said, the salt mines tomorrow."

"It was good to see you again, Mark. I'll be in touch. Oh, wait, call my cell, 971-555-3922, so I'll have your number."

Mark did so and heard the ringing pattern from the living room. "OK, Ben, you have my number. Good to see you again." In his Subaru Mark considered the jaggedness of one person remembering another much better than that other person ever remembered the first.

But then Ben's family had always had much more money than Mark's. Mark was surprised to find himself still fawning over Ben. And he was going to croak where he'd grown up.

The next morning Mark asked, "Do we have anything planned for right after Christmas. Maybe the twenty-eighth or so?"

Maria walked over to a calendar. "No, nothing between Christmas and New Years. And that reminds me, we don't even have plans for New Years anymore."

"We don't?"

"The O'Conners had to cancel their party. Her mother is dying. Joan left for Atlanta this morning."

"Oh. That's disappointing."

"It is for her mother. And Joan."

"I mean—"

"Oh, I know what you mean, Mark. Come on. Maybe we can go somewhere for New Years. But, I sidetracked you."

"Oh. Well, I saw Ben Lehman last night. We went to school together. Remember? You met him at Harry Doyle's wedding. His family lived in that huge house on Claymoor, the Tudor."

"Oh yeah. Chimney pots."

"It's been vacant and dark since Mr. Lehman died.

Last night I saw lights on and a Porsche in the drive, figured Ben was there, and, well, just knocked on the door."

"Really? That's not like you."

"No, it isn't," Mark agreed. "But, anyway, he's going to have a party, a holiday party. And he invited us. He'll let us know the date."

"A bit last minute, don't you think?"

"Yes, but…." Mark trailed off, pointing at the calendar.

"Last minute? Why not. I didn't know you knew Ben that well. Heck, I'm impressed. That's some big money."

"I didn't see him much at all after school. I don't think I've seen him since Harry's wedding. He made some kind of internet killing."

"Hmm. Well, I think I'm looking forward to this!"

Mr. Quinn, of Miller, Fairchild and Quinn, had been managing Ben's father's affairs for two years – paying the bills, arranging for maintenance and insurance and taxes and so on. The Quinn in the law firm's name was Mr. Quinn's uncle, so Quinn the nephew was tossed the lackluster duties involved with handling the needs, wants and whims of clients. Junior held a third-tier law degree, although he had managed a cum laude. He had not much interest in actual applied jurisprudence, really, and sometimes enjoyed his relationships with those who couldn't or wouldn't bother with the details of ordinary living. He was good at contracts and often advised the firm's clients out of unwise pedestrian decisions in a sort of unbilled-hours way many of those he dealt with appreciated. Still, he knew Quinn the uncle was eager and in fact anxious now to get on with settling Ben's father's estate. Junior suggested he might act as a go between in approaching and nudging Ben. After a moment of thought his uncle agreed.

Ben's father, by coincidence, had a reasonably hefty account at Latitude Funds. Two days after Mark and Ben's nocturnal reunion, and four days before Christmas, Mr. Quinn called Latitude regarding documents for probate. Mark was handling some calls for Bill Martin, the manager for the Lehman account, while Bill was on vacation. Bill's secretary put Mr. Quinn's call through to Mark. "My name is Arthur Quinn. My firm is handling Mr. Lehman's estate, Walter Lehman. There are general statements from his account I need."

"Well, Mr. Quinn, Mr. Lehman's account manager is away, so I'm handling some of his calls. I'd be happy to help. Actually, I once knew the family. I just happened to see Ben two nights ago."

"Oh? Where, if I may ask?"

"At the house. Anything I can do to help, I'll be glad to."

"Ben is in town?"

"Yes."

"I see."

The Lehman account was more involved than Mark knew. He needed some POA signatures on a few forms, and so asked Mr. Quinn to come in, which he did the next day. At the end of the meeting Mark said, "I want to thank you for being so prepared. It's not usual, even for many lawyers."

"Well, I don't much like entitlement, Mr. Harris."

"But you deal with it every day, I'd guess."

"True. That's why I don't like it. May I shut your office door?"

"Please."

As Mr. Quinn was returning to his seat he began, "It really is true, you know – you can't go home again. But that doesn't mean people won't try, and they do. I see it often. I once heard someone call nostalgia the heroin of the old. I laughed a little when I heard that. In what I do I've noticed two kinds of nostalgia. One is simply reliving for a little time, in a familiar setting with others who were there, old memories. Fond times. That's fine. We wouldn't be human without that tendency. The other though, that's the heroin. The other is a present attempt to build experiences never had in the first place.

And that is sad. Tragic is the word."

"I can understand that," Mark agreed. He had never considered nostalgia in such a way, finding the idea both intriguing and slightly unsettling.

"The more money a person has, the more that person can pursue the first example into the second. I've seen that happen to regrettable ends, and someone doesn't have to be all that old, either. It's funny. People who have never known significant surplus income, and especially people who've never had enough income to just live, well, they tend to think all rich people are smart and wise. I know blithering idiots with eight-digit trust funds. Some of them would pay for someone else to wipe their rear end if that someone else could be found, if you'll forgive my bluntness. I don't mean in some sort of psychosexual way. That would be an improvement, it would show some initiative regardless of the direction. I mean because they're just that lazy. And, really, in one or two cases, anyway, I'm probably not exaggerating."

Mark thought for a moment in curiosity. "Ben?"

"Oh no, not at all. Not Ben. He made some good decisions, but mostly he was lucky. And he couldn't have been lucky without the money he inherited from his grandfather. Still, he did something with it instead of just spend it dry. That takes attention and some work. How have you known Ben, if you don't mind me asking? I should tell you I intend to use Ben to get his father's estate settled. His siblings, wherever they are, are of no real help. If he's here I'm going to take advantage of that. I don't mean to sound calculating, but this is an opportunity."

"Of course. I understand. We went to school together, for twelve years. We grew up near each other."

"Highland Country Day?"

"Yes. But you know, when we met again the other night, well, I'll just tell you I simply stopped and knocked on the door in the night, I guess 10:30, twenty years later, and that's not like me. I'm not sure why I did that. And when I was leaving, well, I realized I knew him more than he ever knew me. I swam in his pool. We didn't have a pool."

"Yes, chasing the gold ring, with the hope something will rub off. That's why widows living in four-room apartments, wondering if they'll outlive their resources, are Republicans. Or vote for them, anyway," Mr. Quinn laughed. "Did you attend the funeral?"

"No, I had been away for a few weeks. I didn't know about the death until more than a month later. I'm afraid I didn't acknowledge it. I didn't know how to, really, since I had no addresses, hadn't kept up."

"Then you don't know Ben did not attend."

"Really? No, I didn't know."

"I'm not too sure what his absence was about, although I have an idea. He…. Well, I'm afraid I'm wandering into lack of discretion, Mr. Harris. Perhaps I already have. And I'm using your time."

"Not at all. And, please, if you would call me Mark."

"All right, then, Mark. I will."

As Mr. Quinn walked from his office Mark began to wonder about the larger implications of the non-responding siblings. Didn't they at least want the money, even if they didn't need it?

About two hours later Ben called. "Can you make it on the twenty-ninth, Mark?" Mark said they could.

Mr. Quinn called Mark the next day. "Mark, I need a few more statements for the Lehman case. I was hoping you could gather them and run them over. Our offices are not too far. I'd like to use our staff notary, so if you could do this a great deal of back-and-forth could be saved."

Mark, along with Bill Martin's secretary, used two hours in gathering the various forms and statements. When Mark arrived at the offices of Miller, Fairchild and Quinn, which sported a mahogany entrance with a broken pediment along a sleek hall in a Bauhaus high rise, he was greeted in the reception area by a severe-looking woman. "Mr. Harris? I was hoping you would be here earlier. Well, I'll buzz Mr. Quinn."

Fifteen minutes later Mr. Quinn strode in. "Hello

Mark. If I could have the papers we'll get them signed and notarized."

"Everything is here, in chronological order. I'll need to take back copies of the signed originals. Company policy."

"Yes, well, I'll see what we can do." The elder Quinn walked into the reception area. "Oh, Uncle, this is Mark Harris. He's been helping me with the Lehman estate. He's with Latitude. Actually he was a friend of the family."

"Oh?"

"Well, mostly of Ben."

"Harris? Was your father Edmund Harris? Now there was a keen businessman. And a good huntsman."

"Uh, no. Edmund was my uncle. My father was Morgan Harris."

"Oh yes. Yes."

The night of the party at Ben's. Maria had taken her favorite suit of Mark's to be cleaned and pressed, and she selected the tie. She was able to grab a last-minute hair appointment. Mark figured they should go in her Lexus 300, even though it was noticeably older than the Subaru. He had it washed.

As they pulled from their drive Mark said, "I had some very good times at the Lehmans. Especially the summers. When Ben started driving Mr. Lehman still had this Lincoln convertible, with the suicide doors. Man, the places we went. It's a little strange going back over there."

"I really didn't know you were such good friends. It seems I would, after all these years."

"Well, I guess. But maybe I was more his friend than he was mine. I don't know. I think he remembered Linda more than me. She would never go out with him. I never knew why."

"I had a friend like Ben in college. One of those third-tier Kennedy's. I was so eager to get into her circle. It's a little embarrassing now, as I think back. Still, I guess we think some kind of pixie dust from whomever it is will land on us."

"Yep. I know what you mean. You know, one Fourth of July Ben asked me over to shoot off fireworks. I was about fourteen. I rode my bike over, but when I got there his mother told me he'd gone up to their lake cabin with his brothers. I was a little crushed, really. I rode back in the dark. I remember I didn't have a light. But, we were kids."

"Yes, well, a long time ago."

They drove on. "Maria?"

"Yes?"

"Do you mind living in the house I grew up in?"

"Well, no. Not at all. I love our house. Why?"

"Oh, no reason. I was just thinking maybe I should have stayed in Dallas."

"You hated Dallas. We hated Dallas"

"I know. But I think I would be making more than I am, had I stayed with the bank. Maybe a lot more."

As they approached the Lehman house Mark could see only the entrance hall lit. There was no Porsche in the circular drive. "We're not early, are we?" Maria asked.

"No. Not at all. I wonder where everyone is?"

A small, plain wreath from the supermarket was on the door. Mark pushed the doorbell and could hear the chimes clearly. After thirty seconds he pushed again. "Hmm. This *is* Wednesday."

"The twenty-ninth."

Mark walked along the drive to the living room windows. The hall light was enough to let him spot an undecorated tree, not even in a stand, leaning in a corner near the fireplace. He went back to the door, trying the bell a third time.

"Mark," Maria began delicately, "I don't think there's a party here tonight."

After a pause that held a little sigh Mark said, "No. I guess not."

As they were getting in the Lexus an older Mercedes pulled into the driveway and up to the nose of the Lexus.

Both Mark and Maria stood behind their opened doors. The Mercedes stopped and Mr. Quinn and a woman got out. "Mr. Quinn! I see you were invited too."

"Oh," Mr. Quinn said awkwardly. "Actually, no, Mark. Um, this is my wife, Andrea." Andrea nodded.

"Maria, this is Mr. and Mrs. Quinn."

They exchanged nodding pleasantries. "It doesn't seem much is happening here tonight," Maria said.

"Um, no," Mr. Quinn said. "Actually, Ben left this morning, you see. I'm here to pick up some papers he signed for me." Sensing the need for diplomacy Mr. Quinn continued, "As I understand it Ben had been thinking of having a small party. But, change of plans, you see. Unavoidable." That Mr. Quinn was thinking *which apparently Ben didn't bother to tell you* was evident enough in his eyes.

"Oh," Mark said, for at that very moment it was all he could say. Then, "Well, look, if you won't be here too long, maybe you'd like to have dinner with us. As our guests, of course. We've always enjoyed the Bellpost House. It's not far."

A quick wave of surprise took Mr. Quinn's face. "Thank you. But I'm afraid we're on our way to an engagement. We detoured a bit so I could pick up some papers Ben left for me. Well, as I said."

"Perhaps another time," Mrs. Quinn added efficiently.

"Yes," Maria returned quickly. "Well, we'd better be going Mark." Mark did not move to get into the car, but stood as a man will when hoping a few more seconds passing will change the balance. Maria looked at her husband intently, directing, "Mark. Let's go."

Mark and Maria drove home in silence. Maria touched her new hair and looked at Mark in his pressed suit. In their own driveway now Mark said, "Maybe I'll go to Chico's and get a pizza. Is that all right with you?"

"Sure! That sounds good. I'll go in and start a salad. I'll lay a fire. I'll see you in about forty-five minutes?"

"Shouldn't take any longer."

Mark backed his wife's Lexus out of the driveway of the house of his boyhood. He began wondering what used Porsches ran. He was not interested in going to a public place for New Years.

He would pass the Bellpost House on his way to Chico's. As he did he saw Ben's Porsche in the parking lot, Mr. Quinn's Mercedes next to it.

That Mr. Quinn. He handles all the angles.

Next Door

She knew he swam naked at night.

Not that she had ever seen his buttocks or his man parts in distortion, from that second-floor window. Or any anatomy stretched and flickering through long slips of water that, when lit in darkness, seemed to live together like giant transparent worms.

His pool was well enough screened by green and dense verticality, so whether day or in night any view of the pool was nothing more than a knothole in the living fence.

Submerged light moving out through 20,000 gallons of chlorinated water was projected up and away from the pool as if by a psychotic disco ball. No mirror square analog was specific in shape or duration, and the resulting chaos shone onto the walls of upper floors and under eaves, including hers on that side, to some extent. Some might find the display frenetic, she understood, but she found it beautiful and the sort of small detail in daily life movie stars must have.

He sometimes entertained outdoors at night. She

could go into the room with that window and through one of the knotholes catch flashes of people eating pasta and shrimp on glass-topped tables. Of people swimming, or just bobbing in the water or floating on blue rafts as they laughed. If the window was open she could hear directly the din – yet alluring to her – of people with friends so casually being … casual.

But she knew he was swimming naked the nights the pool light was out and his movement through the water was the only sound.

She was out of touch and she knew it, to the extent of wondering if *out of touch* reflected accurately enough her anachronistic tendencies. Her grandchildren once made fun of her and she knew that, too. If only they still would.

She could send and receive email, about the extent of her Internet presence. She had cable only for the purpose of Turner Classic Movies. *How Green was My Valley* was on this night. She had a basic cell flip phone, which often didn't leave the kitchen counter. She drove a primo '98 Park Avenue with sixty-eight thousand on the clock.

Anyway, she once approached the people on the other side of the swimmer, the Warrens. *What did they think of him and that pool he put in and the way he carries on?* and they returned to her, honestly and without affectation, looks of confusion and veiled disbelief.

She no longer knew anyone in Westview Lake, other than the Warrens, and even so only as neighbors. The Warrens bought their house from the estate of Edie Dunlop three years ago. Then Mr. Hardy closed on next door not one week before Harriet Smithers died at Palmer Glen Assisted Living, her house unoccupied for more than two years. When Harriet passed on the loss was not the jolt Mrs. Wilkens expected, curiously. Bill Dunlop went first, then Jack Smithers, then Edie, then Harriet. Actually, within the three couples her Harry had gone first, well before any of the others. All had long and strong Westview Lake roots. They all had been good Westview people.

Although Mr. Hardy had been next door for almost a year, she barely knew him. She doubted they spoke, in any brief way at all, even a half dozen times. She tried to welcome him with a plate of brownies but could never get an answer, so she left the plate at the back door with a note. No acknowledgement came, and now she was out a plate. He was away quite a bit, she noticed … but still.

Harriet and she had been the last original residents and now she, alone, was the last. She once knew almost everyone in the neighborhood – honestly now, almost everyone! – and Harry was mayor from '70 to '74 and she started the garden club and was still president when the club won that beautification award for the main entrance to Westview Lake. How was it possible that one hundred thirty-nine homes could have changed hands since then?

Oh, you do remember when Ed Bigler brought home that beautiful white '68 Eldorado, don't you?

She sat by the telephone in her bedroom for a full hour one uncertain morning before dialing the non-emergency number for the Coventry Hills Police Department, which patrolled Westview Lake under contract.

In early afternoon Officer Jason Miller rang her bell. When she opened the door she did think, but only for a moment, that a young boy dressed up as a policeman stood before her. "Mrs. Wilkens? I'm Officer Miller, of the Coventry Hills P.D. I understand you have a concern you'd like to discuss. May I come in?"

"Oh. Oh yes, please do!" She led him to the living room and offered him a chair. Once seated his gaze instructed her to continue. "Officer Miller, this, this is...."

"Yes ma'am?"

"This is a rather delicate subject. For me. You see, my neighbor, well he...."

"Mrs. Wilkens, whatever the subject is, please believe me, I've seen it all. I've heard it all."

"You have?"

"Yes ma'am. I sure have."

"Here? In Westview Lake?"

"Yes ma'am. In Coventry Hills, and right here in Westview. Mrs. Wilkens, you'd be surprised what I've seen. Especially at four o'clock in the morning."

"Oh dear!"

"Yes. So, whatever your concern is, I'm sure I can handle it. Something about your neighbor? Dr. Hardy?"

Doctor Hardy? He's a doctor? "Officer Miller, he swims naked."

"He does."

"Yes he does. At night."

"Well, how do you know? The reason I ask, Mrs. Wilkens, is that I'm familiar with Dr. Hardy's property. It's pretty well screened, in the summer, anyway. Especially on your side, a solid row of hornbeams. I'd say they're nearly twenty feet tall."

"Yes. But there are a few holes between the leaves, after all. Here and there."

"Well, yes, I guess there would be a few. Is this always at night?"

"Yes."

"So in the pool light, and through the gaps, you've seen … something?"

"Oh no. He swims in the dark. That's how I know he's doing it, when the pool light is off."

"Well, how do you know that's what he's doing?"

"How do I know? Why else would he turn off the light?"

"I see," Officer Miller replied. He took a moment to consider. "Well, I'll grant you swimming naked is somewhat eccentric, if that is in fact what Dr. Hardy is doing. But he's in his own pool. And it seems to me Dr. Hardy has taken more than reasonable precautions to not offend anyone, if, again, he is swimming naked."

After bearing the silence that followed Officer Miller's last words she said, "Well, then, it sounds to me like you're not going to do anything."

"There's nothing I can do, Mrs. Wilkens. Even if what you say is true, and it may be, I don't think Dr. Hardy has broken any law, or even a neighborhood regulation. As I said, if he is swimming naked he's doing so in a private setting. We've never had any complaints about Dr. Hardy, about this in particular or anything else. From what I've heard, to be quite honest, he's good neighbor who takes an interest in the community. Last month he gave advanced CPR instruction to all our officers, with a focus on children and drowning."

"No," Mrs. Wilkens considered, "no I guess he really hasn't broken any laws. And he is in a private setting, I agree. But what it is, Officer Miller…. Well, I think the thing is just knowing what he's doing bothers me. I find *that* offensive and troubling."

"I take your point," the officer said, although he did

not, not really. "Still, it's a pretty thin complaint. I mean, I do want to be honest with you. I'll tell you what, Mrs. Wilkens, I'll make a note of this in my own file. But right now, that's all I can do."

"Well, thank you for coming, Officer Miller."

"Yes ma'am. Goodbye now."

As she shut the door she regretted making the call, figuring the note he would make would be more about her than that Tarzan next door.

That night she called a nephew, a doctor in the next town. "Oh yes, I've heard of him. Came from Denver about a year back," he reported to his aunt. "I've met him a couple of times. His work can be miraculous. Well, he saves children, so of course what he does seems miraculous. He's a pediatric cardiologist. Strange bird, though, I've heard. He keeps his professional life and his private life completely apart. And he wasn't recruited. He just came here, looking for a job, which almost never happens with his level of specialty."

The situation lost some edge for Mrs. Wilkens when her sister in Scottsdale asked her to come visit. Then before she returned Dr. Hardy left for one of those remote lakes in Canada, and then autumn erased the problem, or postponed it, anyway. With the hornbeam leaves falling she watched the pool man stretch the green mesh cover over the pool for the winter. Enough months would pass between today and the pool man's return to let her, as the new year moved on, pretend her problem had gone away. Officer Miller waving to her here and there and from time to time had lingered from the previous summer, and she wished he'd stop.

The observation window was in the side wall of a back bedroom. She was in that bedroom looking for a spool of yellow thread when she heard voices around the pool and looked to see the pool man and his assistant as they lifted off the green cover. With a start she was reminded in full of the problem, and then reminded even more that it was not *the* problem or even *a* problem, but only her problem. Six inches of wet snow in early April had broken away a few hornbeam limbs, and so *her* problem now seemed more so.

The next morning his past unseen nudity was her first thought. Within minutes the entire situation became too much.

After breakfast she watched Dr. Hardy drive away, waited a full minute, and then made her way to the side gate of his privacy fence between the two houses. She had guessed through the leaves that he came to this corner to turn the pool light on or off. Once inside the gate she saw the metal box with a round flap, and under the flap was a switch. She pushed it up, but the day was too sunny. The pool light was in the deep end, the end closest to her back yard. She kept against his house as she moved along the rear wall until she could catch sight of the lens over the bulb, which was in fact on.

For two full weeks after her reconnoitering no night swimming happened. Dr. Hardy kept the light on anyway, for effect she guessed, and so she figured he too favored that Hollywood look. That must be the reason. The light had gone dark at exactly ten thirty every night, so it was on a timer. But on the night of the fifteenth day the light was clicked off manually at ten ten.

For a while she simply sat on her terrace and listened to him move his body through the water.

As she approached the gate she could see his dark movement in the ambient light of the night – the refracted porch lights and landscape lights and street-lights of the neighborhood. In whole she didn't want to do what she was going to, but the part of her that would had already made the decision.

She raised the flap, put her finger on the switch, then looked at the pool. A lattice between the pump shed and the pool deck allowed for some amount of cover. Up.

Light filled the water. Dr. Hardy stopped where he was but, to her surprise, he was not frantic. He bobbed in the shallow end in the farthest corner from her, his legs scissored under him, and she could see he was, in fact, naked. She spied a splotch of dark hair surrounding his parts, which, although submerged, were floating in the density of the water. "Who's there?" he asked, but in a tone that held little concern. Then in words that were playful enough to be not much of a question, "Hey Laurie, is that you?"

She had of course imagined an altogether different reaction from Dr. Hardy, her own reaction had she – somehow – been in Dr. Hardy's spot and found herself under sudden naked illumination. His expected reaction of vulnerability was to have given her the advantage. When she did not find that reaction she was now at the disadvantage. She was, in fact, trespassing and if she could see him he could probably see her enough, especially if she left the enclosure of the lattice and the shed wall in the light. She fumbled to raise the flap. She pushed the switch down.

"Hey!" Dr. Hardy yelled with no playful tone. "Who's there? Who is that?" She was already out the gate, barely comprehending what she had done, mind-spanking the part of her that had. She assumed he would not follow her naked, giving her a little time.

She had refused to become an old woman and took

care to move against that gravity. She had a corner lot and so her driveway was off the side street, and she moved quickly and with sure feet across her front lawn as close to her house as possible, around to the garage side and in through the service door. For some reason she had turned every light off before her mission, and now kept that darkness. Now the best course was to go to bed and pretend that's where she'd been for the last hour.

But she couldn't go to bed. She crept into the back bedroom with the spy window. The pool was dark. She heard no footsteps of investigation. She moved her eyes close to the windowpanes to glean some clue just as the pool light came on again. She jumped back, knocking over her sewing table.

She did get in bed, again wishing Officer Miller wouldn't wave at her.

When her doorbell rang she had been dressed for an hour but not gone downstairs. She was expecting the button to be pushed this morning – of course she was, she wasn't stupid – but still when she heard the chimes she jumped as she sat on the edge of her bed. She looked out the upstairs hall window to see a white unmarked Explorer on the street in front of Dr. Hardy's.

As she reached the foot of the stairway she saw Officer Miller through the sidelight, but when she opened the door another officer stood directly before her. "Mrs. Wilkens," Officer Miller said, "this is Chief Baker."

"Ma'am," the chief said, nodding his head. His smile was honest. "We're investigating a disturbance last night, next door. At Dr. Hardy's."

"Nothing serious," Officer Miller took up. "We think it was just some kids fooling around with his pool light."

"Oh. Oh dear. Well, please come in." She wondered now if her name had slipped from a casual entry in Officer Miller's personal notes into an official departmental file.

"We're hoping you might have seen or heard something last night, around ten fifteen, ten twenty. Between your houses. Maybe a couple of kids."

"Well, no," Mrs. Wilkens said. She wondered if she should have begun with *well.* "I was tired last night, you see. I went to bed around nine thirty. Sometimes I don't go to sleep right away, even when I'm tired. But I think I was probably asleep by then. Two boys, would you say?"

"One was most likely a girl. The ground is a little muddy by the switch. We found a good imprint. A woman's SporTexx, about size eight."

Mrs. Wilkens almost became wide eyed for a moment. Her shoes were still outside the service door where she had left them last night, not wanting to track mud into the house.

"You know, it's amazing, Mrs. Wilkens," Chief Baker said. "Officer Miller simply took a photo of the imprint with his smart phone and uploaded the image. The type of shoe was identified almost immediately as a SporTexx. The women's shoes have a different sole pattern from the men's. So we figure at least one person was an older girl."

"Was there another print? A boy's?"

"No, just the one. But kids almost never engage in pranks alone."

"No, no I guess they don't." She thought she should offer refreshments, but if they accepted they would linger. "Was, was Dr. Hardy in the pool at the time?"

"He wasn't too clear about that. But based on his agitation, I would guess yes," Officer Miller said.

"You know," Mrs. Wilkens said directly to Chief Baker, "he swims in the dark frequently. He … well…."

"Yes. Officer Miller informed me of your concerns, which have been noted, Mrs. Wilkens, I assure you."

"Well, thank you."

The Chief paused to begin a more relaxed tone. "Well now, I understand you're the last of the originals, in the neighborhood."

"Hmm? Oh, yes. Yes I am. The very last, now, since my neighbor Harriet died. Mrs. Smithers. Mr.—Dr. Hardy bought her house and put in that pool. We built this house in 1963."

"I guess the neighborhood has really changed over the years."

"Oh indeed it has," she confirmed. She thought of the gay couple over on Westmont and the Buddhist prayer flags strung between columns on Ashton and the two babies adopted from Nigeria who lived on Lakeshore. She heard Mayor Williams sported a tattoo and she knew the smell of burning marijuana, thank you very much, that sometimes came from back corners of back yards. She also knew some tokers were parents, not just their kids. "I don't really know anyone anymore, I'm afraid. But when our children were coming up, this was such a vibrant neighborhood. Kids coming and going. Bikes and balls in the yards. You don't really see that these days. The toys in the yards. People don't seem too interested in the outside, not so much anymore. Even the kids. My husband and I raised three, two girls and a boy. There's a creek at the bottom of the hill across the street, with a little waterfall. Woods, outcroppings of rock, adventure for a child. Sometimes in the summer, back then, on a Friday or Saturday night, right at dusk, you'd hear the kids running and laughing. You could smell the cookouts and the trees were full of fireflies. On some of those days it truly did seem that Westview Lake was the center of the world. It really did. I remember my children as seeing the neighborhood as a wonderland … but, then, maybe my memory is a little embellished.

Anyway, officers, I could go on, but I'd rather not make a spectacle of myself."

"Yes ma'am. Well, if you should think of anything just let us know."

"Oh I will. Thank you for coming. With people just outside my house last night, our houses, I feel safer knowing you're looking into it."

Mrs. Wilkens stood at her front door and waved. She watched the two officers enter their SUV, then dashed for the service door to get her shoes, putting them in a grocery bag and then hiding the bag in the vacuum cleaner closet. She wondered if she had left a muddy trail last night, but the mud was on the uppers, so the grass must have cleaned the soles quickly enough. Besides, even if muddy tracks were on her grass wouldn't the older girl and her boyfriend have run in front of her house in their escape?

Not ten minutes later the bell rang again. Again she was not surprised, and pretty well knew this caller would be Dr. Hardy. Any refusal to open the door would be a de facto signed confession.

"Mrs. Wilkens I'm Dr. Nick Hardy. Your neighbor."

"Of course."

"I'm sure the officers told you of last night's disturbance and, well, I figured it was high time we were introduced, with more than a wave, anyway, and became proper neighbors. And, I believe this is yours." He offered the plate that once held the brownies. "They were delicious, by the way. I have no excuse for not acknowledging your neighborly gesture. No excuse at all, I'm afraid, other than to say I am truly sorry."

"Oh, well, I, I...." Mrs. Wilkens flubbed out. "Well, I'd forgotten all about the plate. I'm glad you enjoyed them. I left out the pecans. Nuts. You never know."

"No, you don't. Now I was wondering, Mrs. Wilkens, if you might join me for lunch in about two hours. It is such short notice, but would you? I'm afraid it will need to be a bit early."

She wished he hadn't asked, but in the interest of buttressing innocence she had little choice but to accept. "Why, yes, Dr. Hardy, I will. And thank you."

Somewhat after eleven, then, Mrs. Wilkens found herself at the doctor's front door, the only Westview front door she had faced, besides her own and the Warren's, since Harriet had last answered this very door. What if he answered the door naked? What if—"Please come in, Mrs. Wilkens. I thought we could have our lunch on the sun porch." She saw he had spent a bundle on decorating, and she could tell he had told a decorator to "do something and send me the bill."

On the sun porch she sat down in a painted wicker chair. Already in place was her lunch – that organic acorn squash soup from a carton, some chicken salad on a lettuce leaf, iced tea. "My, this all looks so delicious."

"Please, sit down Mrs. Wilkens."

"I heard you came here from Denver, Dr. Hardy."

"Oh?"

"That's what my nephew told me. He's an orthopedic surgeon in Owington. Dr. Andrew Wilkens."

"Andrew Wilkens. Orthopedist? Wait. Oh yes. I met him at a FEMA readiness meeting about six months ago. Nice fellow. But, you know, Mrs. Wilkens, I invited you to lunch not only so we could get together properly but, well, also to perhaps clear things up. A confession, of sorts. You see, I like to swim in the nude." He did not go on.

She had just swallowed a bite of chicken. "Oh?" she coughed, requiring sips of tea. "What an unusual ... hobby."

"I probably wouldn't call it a hobby. It's just that I find it incredibly relaxing and exhilarating at the same time. Somehow I do. I'm a pediatric cardiologist. I deal with sad stories every day, and swimming that way, in the buff, well, it helps put the sadness behind me. On certain days, anyway. It ... well, I guess it makes me feel like Tom Sawyer." He smiled as a boy would. "But, anyway, I want you to know it's a solitary practice. And I always turn out the light. I wouldn't want to cause anyone discomfort. I've never told anyone but my girlfriend, but I guess word somehow got out and those kids last night, well, they were just being kids."

"Yes, just that. I'm sure that's all it was."

"Still, I might like to get my hands on them," he continued, looking directly at her.

"Oh?" she replied, almost with a quiver.

"Well," he smiled again, "simply an expression. That's all."

"I see. Well, now, at any rate, I think I can see how swimming in that state would allow you to shed some burdens. I—"

"Yes. Well put, Mrs. Wilkens."

"Yes. But, I was thinking, I suppose most folks don't think of children as having heart problems."

"No they don't. You're quite right. But kids do, maybe more than anyone might guess. The specialty requires odd hours. Sometimes all I do here is sleep. Sometimes not even that. Sometimes I sleep in the doctors' lounge. But I love it. I wouldn't want to do anything else. I think I'm making a difference. I know I am. So, then, Officer Miller tells me you've lived next door fifty years!"

"Yes. Fifty years this December, upcoming. I won't tell you what we paid, back then."

"Please don't," he laughed. "I know I'll ever get back what I've put into this place. But then, that sort of consideration has never concerned me. I've found most people underestimate the implicit value in pleasure. Pure pleasure."

Not too soon for Mrs. Wilkens she ate a small éclair from a grocery deli case and then made her goodbyes. As she walked back to next door she felt like an item that had been checked off a list.

The summer wore on, and many nights Dr. Hardy's pool light was off. She figured Officer Miller was right. Whatever Dr. Hardy did next door was his business, and he kept his business discreet, and he had been honest with her about it.

August held cool, often damp nights and now she could just see the gas flame between vents in the bottom of the pool heater housing. Sweltering July afternoons relieved by cool water had flipped into cool August nights in which the embrace of warmer water was sheltering. Now the night swimming was starting later and continuing longer, often well past midnight. The water sounds were not troublesome to a reasonable neighbor, unless they were being listened to and not just heard. That his nighttime diversion was no longer solitary was clear. Lately she was hearing a woman's voice and from time to time that woman's laugh. Some nights she noticed quiet stretches when the water sounds stopped and she wondered if they were having intercourse on top of a blue foam raft on the concrete deck, or perhaps even vertically in the water. Mrs. Wilkens assumed the Laurie he had called out to the night of her incursion was the source of the feminine voice and laughter. The light remained off during the splashing and giggling.

On a moonlit night in that month she was at the window, trying to see any sort of activity through the trees. She was looking at the far end of the pool, then as she returned her sights to the close end there stood Dr. Hardy on the pool deck, looking up at her window through a gap in the trees. Her body shook, but rather than pull back she froze. She was certain he stood in the moonlight deliberately, as well as nakedly.

The next afternoon a box was delivered to her silently, anonymously. The box contained a pair of night-vision binoculars. Officer Miller was her first thought, but she couldn't call him, she just couldn't, the situation had already gone too far. She pulled down the shade in the window and left it down, hoping the gesture would send the right message. She tried to pretend none of this had happened.

More than a week later the shade was still down. Surely Dr. Hardy understood the meaning of the blocked window, that she had no further interest in his goings on, not that she ever really had. Not really, no.

She had always been an accurate judge of character, generally. The skill was visceral, but often the gut knowledge would be proved by evidence, if only eventually, and so she had most often kept her judgments to herself.

And she knew doctors had access to drugs, of course. Many doctors had lived in Westview Lake over the decades and from her own experience she also knew doctors, sometimes very good ones, could have private lives completely disjointed from their practices. Still, she shuddered as she wondered what sort of carnal tangents might be going on over there, when that light was out.

She was unable to put from her mind the binoculars, of course, and she chided herself for being manipulated away from witnessing her neighbor's activities, because to her mind something over there did, for the greater good, need witnessing. Still, she did witness with her ears sometimes, simply by being on her terrace as a normal part of her night, and caught sounds moving through the hedge. Not only the sounds could be strange, but more so the juxtaposition of those sounds, sounds of some desperation then followed by laughter and glee and just plain silliness.

At the market a day or two later, pushing her cart down the produce aisle, a stunningly beautiful young woman called out, "Mrs. Wilkens!" She recognized the voice as Laurie's. "Mrs. Wilkens I'm Laurie White. I'm Nick's friend. Dr. Hardy."

"Oh yes! From the other side of the hedge."

"Yes. That's right. But, you know, I wanted to explain to you – I don't have much time, I'm afraid – explain to you that Nick is under a great deal of stress. People handle stress in different ways, Mrs. Wilkens." She paused and looked down the aisle in the direction of the store's entrance. "My concern, Mrs. Wilkens, is that you may be adding to his stress level, and I wish you wouldn't. I really do. Look, I'll simply say what I need to. What I'm asking you to do, Mrs.—"

"What you're asking me to do, young lady, is for me to mind my own business."

Laurie did not yield to Mrs. Wilkens's stance. "Yes," she replied firmly. "That is exactly what I'm both asking and suggesting. Strongly."

"Already done, Ms. White. To the extent I might have meddled inadvertently, as far as I'm concerned what happens in the Hardy pool stays in the Hardy pool."

"Thank you," Laurie returned, and quite genuinely. But then with another glance down the aisle her confident demeanor faded. Mrs. Wilkens was not surprised to hear Dr. Hardy's voice coming from behind.

"Well well. And what might my two favorite ladies be talking about on this fine afternoon?"

The present dynamic was clear enough to Mrs. Wilkens and she commenced to rescue Laurie. "Why,

Dr. Hardy. I was just telling Laurie what a wonderful host you are and how much I enjoyed our recent lunch together."

"Yes, Nick," Laurie took up, a bit too quickly. "How delicious!"

In the parking lot Mrs. Wilkens spotted Officer Miller cruising through. She motioned him over with a fully extended arm, pulling her fingers towards her but he just waved back with that insipid smile and drove on.

On the way home she was not able to refuse anger. The officer must have known she wasn't simply waving hello, the stupid man. She decided he had understood her gesture but didn't want to be bothered, but that wasn't true.

In her driveway, out of view from the Hardy yard, Officer Miller got out of his cruiser. "Let me help you with those," he said, taking a bag with a floppy toupee of carrot greens, motioning his head towards the house.

In the kitchen he continued. "What's going on, Mrs. Wilkens? I figured you'd rather not talk through my cruiser's window in a parking lot."

"Oh. Well, yes. That," she flustered, needing a moment to move beyond her underestimation of him. "Officer Miller, I know you must think I'm just a lonely, crazy old—"

"No ma'am," he interrupted. "I do not." His tone was convincing.

"Well, then, well then Officer Miller, *something* is going on at Dr. Hardy's. I just know it. Something very odd and not right. The thing is, I don't like using the air conditioner unless it's very hot. It's not about money, I simply don't care for it. So my windows are often open. There are sounds at night, from next door. He's not alone and sometimes the strangest sort of, of guttural sounds are coming from over there, late. Often very late. And there's a woman who's doing things it sounds to me as though she doesn't want to do. Or not always, anyway. You see.... Pardon me, please, Officer Miller, I'm going to show you something." She got up and soon returned with a box from the hall closet. "On a night after the pool light incident, months after, you see, I do admit I was looking through the window. Out of concern, Officer Miller. I was looking down at the far end of the pool. The light was off, of course, but the sky was clear and the moon was exceptionally bright. When I looked back at the end closer to me Hardy was standing there naked. I could see him in the moonlight. And I think he saw me. I know he saw me. He must have, because the next day these were at my front door. I don't know who delivered the box."

Officer Miller took the box from her, opened the flaps. "Wow. Infrared. And expensive." He reached in to pick up the binoculars.

"Stop! I haven't touched them. Fingerprints."

"Right. Good call, Mrs. Wilkens. When was this?"

"About two weeks ago. And this was also in the box. I handled it before I thought not to." She handed him a greeting card, on the front a smug Barney Fife, inside the original message, *Nip it in the bud.* After *Nip* was an editor's arrow leading to *–ping* written in very careful block letters.

When Officer Miller returned his eyes to her his bearing was noticeably changed. "You should have called me."

"I know. I know that. But I wanted to pretend it hadn't happened, that none of this has. Right after I opened the box I went upstairs and pulled down the window shade, the one on the side window in that back bedroom, and it's been down ever since. I hoped he would get the message. Maybe he has."

"Maybe so. Let's hope, anyway." He paused to consider his words. "The thing is, Mrs. Wilkens, the problem is we're pretty much where we were last summer. Unless the woman is an underage girl, or unless illegal drug use is going on, there just isn't much I can do. Actually, there's nothing I can do. The Warrens have not complained, the people in the house directly behind Dr. Hardy have not complained, nor have the folks on either side of the house directly behind. Even if—"

"They never open their windows. Nobody does anymore. That's why no one has complained."

"Yes, I guess they don't. But, still, even if I were to witness the sounds, I don't think I would have probable cause. He's on his own property and, as I said, only you have complained. But, I'll try to keep an eye out, and an ear. Have you noticed anyone coming to his house who doesn't seem to belong?"

She thought across the past days and weeks. "No. No I haven't." She knew Officer Miller was doing all he could, and now appreciated his attentiveness. "I was wondering, just curious, really, did you get anywhere with the kids and the pool light?"

Officer Miller did not respond immediately, although his response was quick enough. Still, just enough time filled his gap to alert her. "Nothing definite. Actually, I'm thinking it might not have been kids at all, or even more than one person," he told her, his closed smile a little too affected. "Well, I'll be on my way. I'm glad you told me about the binoculars, and as I said I'll be on the lookout."

She showed him out, then turned her back against the door as she closed it. She knew, without doubt now, her name had left his private notebook and she was certainly a person of interest in the department's files.

She could not remember ever in her life being a person of interest.

As he had indicated to Mrs. Wilkens when they first met, Officer Miller was indeed familiar with pre-dawn life. While more sporadic in suburbia, its essence was not so much diluted here. He had an idea about the sounds, a pretty good idea, really, upheld by her report of a possible reticent partner. But still no probable cause. In his cruiser, in the simple spiral notebook he carried for his own purposes, Officer Miller made three quick entries:

- intimidation of Mrs. W

- drugs to increase vascular diameter/side effects?

- autoeroticism/assisted?

For two nights not only was the pool not lit, but the house was completely dark, including all the landscape lighting. She noticed Officer Miller pass by slowly at least three times. A car she did not recognize was parked in Hardy's driveway during that time, one of those Chrysler 300s with big wheels and blacked-out windows. On the third night the lights and activity returned. At ten the pool light was switched off.

At about ten thirty she heard straining sounds and moans from next door. Laurie was calling out *Nick* in a trembling voice wet with tears, imploring him. "Nick," she then said softly and matter-of-factly, searching for some angle of control. "Come ON! Stay with me." But her search was useless and her voice again reflected futility. "Nick. Breathe. Breathe! Please, just … do something."

Mrs. Wilkens called Officer Miller on his cell. "This is Jane Wilkens, Officer Miller. I think you should get over to Dr. Hardy's. And quickly."

She then made her way to the side gate, over to the switch. Laurie was too involved to notice her. She put her finger on the toggle at the same moment she began to lose her nerve, but then she saw Officer Miller's blue lights pull to the curb, his response silent. Up.

With the light came a staggered gasp that, once its inhalation was complete, was immediately exhaled in a hoarse scream, a scream not pure and steady like they are in the movies. Laurie stood naked. Dr. Hardy lied naked on his right side, facing Mrs. Wilkens. The staccato light from the pool did not expose the scene much.

Officer Miller came around the driveway side, on the other side of the house from the filter shed and the switch. His flashlight beam mimicked his quick gait as he approached. He stopped and without a question or a word began moving the beam with purpose – to Laurie's face, then to Mrs. Wilkens's face, then, beginning at the feet, along the length of Dr. Hardy, catching his man parts briefly in the beam, stopping on his face. The garrote around his neck had been loosened, his eyes and mouth frozen in a display of complete surprise, an expression that would not change even as Officer Miller looked for signs it might.

Prada Marfa is Open for Business

REPORT – SHERIFF'S DEPARTMENT, JEFF DAVIS COUNTY, TEXAS

Deputy Thompson states at 23:20 hours 3 Sept. 2015 was traveling east on U.S. 90. Passed Prada Marfa art installation, noticed silver Ford Fusion parked beside structure. Small suitcase on back seat. Identifiers indicated the car a rental. Further investigation found four articles of women's clothing in front of structure – one patterned short dress, one pair red underwear, two platform-type shoes. No evidence of forced entry; no subject found in vicinity. As suggested by deputy, car and clothing could be additional artistic statement by creators of installation. Incident was reported to TxDOT.

He always left for work at six in the morning, six days a week. In winter months six was still dark. He thought he was being quiet in his morning routine. She always pretended to be asleep as he left, thankful that he liked to eat breakfast at the Prairieland Diner on the way.

Shoot the breeze.

The gravel would crunch from the knobby truck tires

as he left. She'd sit up and look out the bedroom window. She'd watch the red taillights move down their road, then see the brake lights as he came to a stop at the county road. He always stopped. Not a dozen other cars came down this stretch in a day, but he always stopped fully. Once, she remembered, she thought to ask him why as a way to make three seconds of conversation. These days, three seconds of conversation were not worth the three thousand silent ones that followed.

They never shot the breeze.

Earlier, back when, she'd known the Woman in a Zoo relationship. Her hair kept as that one had wished. The makeup to his liking, as if her face was a yellow cake to be iced with lemon frosting. The clothes he brought in to make her look like Mrs. Elvis, wherever the hell he had gotten them (and she could not imagine where). Bible passages quoted. Physically isolated. A shame she directed on herself.

The remarkable angle on that lockup was his mama springing her, just showing up one mid-morning with real clothes, a suitcase, three hundred in cash and a bus ticket to Nashville. "Look, darlin'," Mama said, "you get a bun in the oven and it's all over. *All* over." Mama was touched by the look of concern in her eyes. "Don't worry, sweetie. I can handle the blowback. I outsmarted his daddy, I can sure outsmart this one."

This deal wasn't like that one. She had full use of a

Subaru Baja. An '04 but with only thirty-four thousand on the clock. Still, living in the middle of the middle of nowhere, thirty miles northwest of Odessa, included lonely like the bark in a dog. She had no friends out here. She hadn't met another woman whose habit of living around these parts didn't go back at least three or four generations. People who grew up around here and stayed simply because their grandparents or great grandparents broke down nearby, somewhere. Once.

She enjoyed watching his taillights become smaller in the morning dark. These days the only deal worse than being alone was being alone together.

She gave up on Facebook 'cause she had nothing to post. For the last few months she deleted her search history every afternoon, before he got home, but that wipe was mostly a game she played with herself, pretending he was interested enough to look. She looked for T & A on his history, probably as part of the same pretend game. She knew up front she'd find nothing to fuel the possible thirty-second conversation or ten-minute argument, but then either would have been something, anyway.

Around four in the afternoons she started supper as that draining evisceration of daily non-accomplishment dragged her down to the drudgery of habit. She often looked at a calendar to know the day of the week, sometimes surprised to find the day was Friday, 'cause wasn't Monday just yesterday? How could Ellen and Dr.

Phil and point and click have filled up the week so?

In Florida he told her the attic bedroom had sky-lights and a west-facing dormer and she could use the space as her studio. Jesus, is that why she'd come to the middle of the middle of nowhere northwest of Odessa? He quit asking for sex a while back, and she'd never been good at suggesting she might want to be intimate. Or just penetrated, even.

Or simply touched.

Marfa was in one direction from Odessa, Archer City, with McMurtry's bookstore, in the other, although about another hour and a half farther. Both had caught her imagination.

Archer City was on the edge of East Texas green, if barely, while Marfa was in the high desert, hardly distinguishable from Mexico. Had geology pushed the Rio Grande northeastward Marfa would be in Mexico.

She was a casual fan of McMurtry's kid's music, about as close to country as she'd go anymore, and that's how they met in Key West. "So, you like James McMurtry?" he asked.

To her he looked and sounded prosperous, and five days later they flew in someone's Beechcraft from Key West over the Gulf and then landing at Schlemeyer Field.

She had a BFA in ceramics from the University of Alabama Birmingham. So, she had toted herself and her degree across the Southeast, looking for dreamy opportunity, unable or unwilling to grasp just how un-groovy life on planet Earth really can be on some days, sometimes maybe most days.

Both the bookstore and the shoe store were shiny for her, then, but almost daily she would look at online photos of Prada Marfa. The little white box made her think, in sort of an opposite or inverted way – kind of like a photo negative – of a lemonade stand on the moon. With front-facing plate glass windows the tiny store looked like an aquarium, maybe, or maybe a terrarium. It looked like a place more about keeping stuff out rather than in. Later she made a cardboard model of the desert folly, and then one from clay.

That she ever got to college, or had even thought of going, or had even thought to think about going, was at the wand tip of her counselor, for magic was as good an explanation as any. The counselor had, week by week for a year and a half, plotted her charge's escape, determined this piney woods girl would not become just a piney woods woman. Determined that she would not decide to not decide, that she would not simply package the first day after high school then repeat that day twenty thousand times, accepting as normal the oddly sweetly acrid smell of the pulp mills.

The counselor had to dodge the Jesus and drunkenness of pineywoodsdom. She had to all but lie to her protégé's parents and guide her in saying not too much. The counselor was not inexperienced with such mazes.

No, she wasn't.

The counselor worked with her to get her grades up and found her scholarships and grants and drove her to Birmingham two days before the first day of the first semester. She got her settled in her dorm room and slipped fifty dollars into her back pocket as the two hugged goodbye and later when her new roommate told her her mother was so nice she did not disagree.

College was an unimagined refuge for her that soon enough eclipsed her freshman anxiety and was like antimatter to pineywoodsdom. She hated going home on holidays and figured out reasons to stay summers.

When she graduated she figured she would be taken by the hand and pointed in the direction that was hers. Or pointed in a direction, anyway. *Ceramics* was not a heading in the classified ads. Her counselor's husband had beaten the hell, crap and living daylights out of his wife right before her graduation from UA Birmingham.

But she did not know what happened to her counselor and so she was pointed in all directions in a spinning sort of way that heeded no compass.

In varying locations, then, across years that zipped from New Years Day to New Years Eve without survey, she teetered weekly, if sometimes not almost daily, between barely able to support herself and just flat out broke, hungry, and cold or hot and lonely. She would understand how an offer to fix those holes had gotten her through the gate into the zoo.

She just kept going south in Florida, that's all. She thought she might open a little shop and sell clay cartoonish turtles and seahorses and starfish to tourists. When she heard, "So, you like James McMurtry?" there in Key West one afternoon she hadn't eaten much since yesterday. She guarded the seven dollars and thirty-three cents in her pocket, figuring she couldn't not eat tomorrow. But she could tell this one wasn't like the other one.

She was right. The other one had paid attention to her, anyway, however much the wrong kind, stroking her like a dog who would rather be alone in the back yard for a while. Still, this one bought her clay, glazes and an old kiln that worked sometimes.

She hadn't been up to her studio in days.

Weeks? How long. Hmmm. Maybe Judge Judy or Sharon Osbourne knows.

Who he had been in Key West had rarely appeared

back home here in Texas. Not that he was occasionally witty in Florida, or vaguely urbane, but he had been something beyond robotic, anyway. Here, he worked the gas fields and after supper was too tired to much do anything. Likely as not he fell asleep in his recliner under TV glow, most nights after supper. Sometimes, or rather once in a while, they'd drive into Odessa for a movie. She tried to get him down to Marfa. "It's like an artist's colony. It'll be fun, you know?"

His drinking could never be anyone's idea of a problem. She hadn't smoked weed for longer than she could figure. Hell, she didn't know where to score, not out here, and not in Odessa proper.

Later she got the kiln to work reliably and did pretty well selling ceramic Christmas ornaments on Etsy and eBay. She was driven upstairs to the studio more by money than a creative itch, but then so much in life happened because it had to, more than any wanting it to, or so seemed whatever this plane is. "Hell," she said one morning, watching the taillights, cocking her head like a dog, "I'm twenty-nine years old." She got out of bed to look in the mirror. "How did that happen?" *What if she got a bun in the oven with this one?* she thought before remembering. Anyway, she liked having money.

Lone Star Prairie Monthly sponsored a contest she entered twenty-two times. Twenty-two envelopes, twenty-two stamps. In early July she found twenty-two unsold Junes in the trash out back of Parnell's Pharmacy. Anyway, she won the grand prize, three days at the Chisos Mountain Lodge in Big Bend.

She was so excited! How he wasn't left her bewildered. "Well, would you go with me just for me? It's free. The food's free. Just some gas money. I'll buy the gas." She did not mention right then that the Prada store was in the overall vicinity of Big Bend. On the way, kind of.

"Maybe." But his answer used five letters to say only no. Hell, he couldn't be bothered to say an actual *no*. He couldn't not mumble the *maybe*, he couldn't not be walking away as he did that mumbling.

"Fuck you," she mumbled back.

"Huh?" he reacted back without comprehension.

"I said ... supper will never be ready."

"OK. I'll be in the shower."

Anyway, she usually didn't have to smell him.

The next evening she said, "OK. Then I guess I'll just go by myself."

"Huh?"

"I'll go by myself."

"Go? Go where?"

"To Big Bend."

"Big Bend?"

"Yes. I won a trip there. You know? Remember? I told you last night."

"Oh. Yeah. Right. I thought that was a joke."

A while back she'd driven the Subaru to Odessa one afternoon to open a checking account at the Wells Fargo there so she could funnel the eBay and Etsy proceeds accumulating on PayPal. About a week after opening the account her debit card arrived in the mail.

She looked at the card, went online to look at her balance, then smiled. Marfa sat three hours away. Booked Up four and a half hours. She'd been set on Marfa, pretty much, but then she found out Prada Marfa wasn't in Marfa, or even what could be called particularly close, but then what could be called, at thirty miles more on from Marfa, close enough, in Texas.

Now she had two equations:

- A fake Prada store on the outskirts of the middle of another middle of nowhere
- A functioning used bookstore in a town smaller than Marfa

Quantitatively the two seemed about equivalent.

Booked Up, though, did seem less like an old Monty Python skit. The Prada store was intended to decay in and by and under and within the desert sun and wind. Booked Up was a living undertaking. With and in Booked Up was initial irony, and now background irony, but the Prada gag was actively ironic.

He wouldn't go to Big Bend. Not for free, not for nothing. She knew he could take off work for a week if he wanted, with pay. But he didn't.

Cook and a maid, that's all. Stove and a mop. She would still pleasure him without return pleasure, she really would, just robot on robot for three minutes, if he wanted. He didn't, of course.

So she walked down the gravel drive to the county road and then down the county road to the federal highway. Facing away from Odessa she stuck out her right thumb, holding a small suitcase. Within five minutes a portly man wearing Under Armor stopped his Hummer 2. "Where you headed, Odessa?"

"Yeah." She waited for him to hit on her but he did not.

In Odessa she rented a silver Ford Fusion. In the bathroom of the agency she changed from jeans and a man's shirt into a little dress with spaghetti straps and she slipped on wedgies. She was already wearing the naughty underwear – red and lacey and crotchless – that had done her no good.

She zipped along I-20 for a while, then moved south on state and federal roads, easy on the gas pedal. Hours later, at the intersection of 385 and 90, she turned west onto 90, with a decision waiting in just about two miles at the dogleg of 385.

When she saw the sign for 385 she pulled onto the shoulder and put the Fusion in park. Now, she had to decide between Marfa – just stay on 90 – or Big Bend, continue south again on 385. Booked Up had, sometime earlier she noticed now, gone from four and a half hours away to being clear to almost Oklahoma. Almost.

Maybe what she needed, maybe all she wanted, was raw irony. Irony, *noun*, root Greek word *eirōn*, meaning dissembler.

Well, bingo, then.

As a girl she wondered what the edge of the universe might look like, thinking the place would be one of white light, and peaceful in a way inviting forever. Mapquest had told a three-hour drive from Odessa proper to Marfa, but she didn't know how long she'd been gone and time was kind of funny now … no, iffy. Yes that's the word.

Thirty miles still on from Marfa put her in Jeff Davis

County, a trapezoid that sports an average of one human per square mile. Prada Marfa is the only building for miles and so when she spotted the white angles of the walls from a good distance she knew what the place ahead had to be. Dusk was well happening, giving low-sky red to the west. She pulled off the road. She got from the silver Fusion and walked to the front of the store, standing about ten feet away. Before disappointment of some flavor could begin, as she feared disappointment and regret might, the lights inside the store popped on and drove back the darkening air in an instant.

In this new light she laughed and giggled and put her fingers to her lips while her eyes widened and sparked for the first time in a long time. Prada Marfa was everything and all she had expected and by the next second was more. Everything and all and more despite not knowing just what to expect – if anything, really, beyond the online photos – all this day and scattered parts of many days before, going back weeks, probably. What at first – but only the very first, thankfully – what at first looked to be a couple of empty U-Store units with the doors up was now a beacon that poured light onto and across the middle of the middle of the middle of nowhere. The racks of shoes were backlit and the handbags sat on little daises and she even thought maybe in some way or another the air inside was pumped in from Milan and didn't smell of dust and cow shit and rotting hay.

She knew what to be an artist was, however long she had denied herself that knowledge in full light. In this very moment she connected with the two artists who not only conceived of Prada Marfa, but dragged it into existence. She delighted in their absurdity and she thought of the *Green Acres* reruns she loved and he despised and of Arnold the Pig and of Lisa Douglas dressed in a negligée as she fed the chickens. She smiled and laughed and jumped into a tiny dance.

The universe ends at or in an infinite number of places, then, and was ending here and surely Prada Marfa was a place of peacefulness and was inviting forever.

She'd read we're mostly empty space, that atoms have not much to them, that electrons are simply statistical charges of probability, that one galaxy can pass through another without their respective stars bumping into one another.

Yes.

Dusk was over. She wanted to be consumed by the emerging light, and was certain she was being so. She removed her clothes, then walked towards the right-hand plate window and when she was upon it the mostly space in and of her body commenced to slide past the mostly space in and of the glass. This process continued until complete and she was inside Prada Marfa, exactly where she had wanted to be for the longest time.

Ten-Buck Trick

As summer wore on, todays flowing into tomorrows with little notice or care, the relief given by night air was harder to find. The temperature at four in the afternoon didn't matter much. The temperature at eleven at night did.

By the second week in July the gap between the later afternoon reading and the almost-tomorrow reading narrowed significantly. As the long run of such days started, then, sundowns would not begin a predictable cooling, only a lessening of heat confirmed by mercury, but not by skin or its sweat, or inhaled air.

Spencer's bedroom was in the attic, with a single window facing east. Wind nearly always arrived from the west, but after the Fourth of July or so that he could not catch breezes barely mattered, for they were hot and offered no ease. On the hottest nights any wind, including the flow from the large fan on his desk, only mocked the state of unfound sleep. A deep eave held his window, and so even in rain it was always open to some level. Only December, January and February would find the bottom sash in place fully.

In the swelter Spencer would lie naked on a sheet. His mother considered his bareness unseemly, especially now that he was thirteen and a half, but he didn't care. She never came upstairs, nobody did, so what did that matter?

The two moved to town when Spencer's mother lost her job as cook on the Circle T Ranch. He did not know the particulars of the loss, only that the event was not just sudden, but jagged beyond that suddenness. They lived on the ranch for six years in a three-room house. Despite finding a job as a receptionist in Doc Brewer's office, appealing to her in both description and pay, she was still sometimes sad, and mad, about being uprooted. Spencer felt not so disrupted, and now found town life alluring. The days were sometimes different and he met children his age and he did not miss the smells of rotting hay and cow shit.

Spencer was a handsome boy with sorrel hair. His teeth were perfectly aligned, a natural gift that set him apart, mostly, in a town two-hundred miles from orthodontics. His body weighed almost one hundred ten pounds, but, at already five feet six, if he told anyone he was fifteen he was believed without much of a second thought. His voice hadn't changed so much, but he never did have much of a child's highness and so that unreached mark could go largely unnoticed.

He might have handled nights of unfound sleep by going downstairs to have a Coke and watch Johnny Carson, but his mother, in a random act of setting limits, determined both diversions to be outside of childhood. She slept soundly. She would not hear the sounds of the refrigerator door, or the TV, but the first several steps of the stairs squeaked like a goddamn mule farting. No, really, they did.

On this night Spencer shined his flashlight at the thermometer outside his window. Although 12:30 a.m., the air temperature was 87°. He pulled on some shorts and a T shirt and slipped his feet into tied sneakers. Directly below his window was a trellis. He popped the eye hooks holding the screen and wriggled out his window. He once tested the trellis from the other direction, judging the stoutness of the crosspieces. Tonight was the first time he applied his findings downward.

Spencer and his mom lived about three blocks from the small downtown. The three-story Ploughman's Bank was the tallest building, although its height was exceeded by grain elevators and water towers. He headed mothlike for the bright lights, such as they were, but before hitting Center Street he heard his name called. He turned, but saw no source. "Over here, Carter," he heard again. He found Tommy lurking behind the drugstore. "Isn't it past your bedtime, kid?"

"Couldn't sleep."

"How'd ya get out?"

"Through my window, down the trellis. What's your excuse?"

"'Bout the same. I've never seen ya here out before. Should I have?"

Spencer took a moment to consider. "Nope. First time."

Tommy opened a small cooler, offering Spencer a cold can. "Want one?"

Half expecting a Lone Star, Spencer was relieved to find a Dr. Pepper in Tommy's hand. "Thanks!"

"God is it ever hot."

"Yeah. I just had to get outta the house."

"Yeah. Your daddy with ya?"

"What?"

"Your daddy. Does he live with you and your ma?"

"Oh. No," Spencer told as fact. Unsure about going on, he did in hopes of bonding with Tommy. "I mean, well, the deal is … I've never met my father."

"Never? Sometimes I wish I'd never met mine. Who

was he?"

"I don't really know. Some ranch hand, somewhere, I guess. I know his name. That's all. Don't even have a picture. I mean, you asked, so I told you."

"OK, but … ya don't have a picture? What about your ma. Doesn't she have one?"

"I guess. Maybe somewhere. But she told me if I ever wanted a picture of him all I need do is look in a mirror."

"Yeah. OK." Tommy threw a rock at a milk crate. "See that light in the sky? It looks like a high up plane comin' in for a landing, but it never moves. And you can see the colors. That's curious."

"It's Sirius. The Dog Star."

"You know that stuff?"

"Well, yeah."

"That's cool." The two then sat in silence, for a length of time that would bother girls of this age. "Well, I'd better be goin'."

"OK. See ya." Spencer looked around town for a bit more. Besides a cat or two, he saw a man coming down the back stairs at the feed store. Ten minutes later another man went up. The climb down the trellis would become something of a habit with Spencer.

Over the next month Spencer discovered a half dozen

boys who liked wandering in the heat of the night. He knew two from school, including Tommy, was acquainted with two, and met two for the first time, although he'd seen them around. One of the new friends, Sam, was, at better than fifteen, the oldest kid in town, or the oldest boy, anyway, the oldest boy boy. Statistical cyclical patterns of birth and migration delivered no boys of sixteen or seventeen. Most of the eighteen- and nineteen-year-olds were off to ag school or the military, or just somewhere – anywhere – else, except for Bradley Graham, who won a full scholarship to Cal Tech to study physics, but he was that way, after all.

As often as not the boys would emerge and meet up in threes on any particular night. As the youngest, Spencer preferred this dynamic. Two wasn't a group, and a trio prevented the inevitable pairing four brought about, and with five or six he became just the tag along. The other boys never really thought about Spencer's age, although he was the only one called by his last name. He wasn't the shortest and he was probably the smartest. During the tit and pussy talk he smiled and laughed at the right times, and at the right times said, "You know it!" and, "Yeah!"

A high pressure cell over the area had not budged during the second week of August, pushing the daytime highs into three digits. Moisture moved in from the Gulf, spiking humidity that, mixed with nighttime lows that were cursed, made sleep otherworldly.

Spencer shined his flashlight. Ninety. A full moon beckoned. He slipped on his shorts and his shoes, too hot for a shirt. He walked to the tracks and put an ear to one, the steel hotter than the night air, still. Nothing was coming. He waved to the deputy, who was well aware of the boys of the night but, to him, anyway, they were harmless. The deputy started his cruiser and drove towards Spencer, stopping. "Hey, Spence."

"Hey Marvin. Seen anyone else?"

"Not tonight. So now, does your mama know where ya' are?" Spencer gave him a look. "Well, yeah. OK."

"Hey, don't worry. I'm headed back."

"OK, then. I'll see ya."

Spencer had walked two blocks towards home when again, in this other late night, he heard his name come from the darkness. "Sam?"

"Yeah, Carter. Over here." Sam was behind the bank.

"I didn't see you earlier."

"I saw you. Didn't want Marvin to see me."

"Oh."

"No train tonight?"

"Didn't hear anything."

"What were you goin' to do, wave at the engineer?"

"Nah. I figured I'd put a quarter on the track."

"Oh?"

"Yeah."

"Seems like a waste."

"Uh-uh. Kid from school, lives over on Parker Street, he buys 'em for fifty cents."

"What kid?"

"Nate Graham."

"Oh yeah. That feeb. And to think he's got that smart brother."

"Yeah."

Sam drew a target in the dirt, then spat at the bull's-eye. "Hey, see that light on in that window, above the feed store there?"

"Yeah."

"That's Charlene Johnson's place. Looks like she's not so busy tonight."

"Busy?"

"Yeah. You know. She's a hooker."

"A hooker?"

"Well, yeah. A whore. A prostitute. Ya know? I mean, ya get that. right?"

"Yes."

"I mean, well, ya know what a whore is, right?"

Spencer looked at Sam with straight lips and lowered eyebrows. "Yes, I know what a prostitute is."

"Thing is, I hear she's a ten-buck trick. Only cost you ten. Anyway, that's what I hear. I mean," Sam continued, raising a level palm into the air, "you don't have to be this tall to ride the ride. I hear she once did a kid who was twelve. Almost thirteen but still twelve."

Spencer turned to Sam in doubt. "Twelve. *Twelve?*"

"Well, yeah."

"Where'd you hear that?"

"Around."

"Yeah? Look, I don't think I believe that. I mean, come on, not only that *she'd* do him, but that a twelve-year-old would, you know, want to."

Sam spat again. "How old are you?"

"Fourteen. Well, thirteen and a half."

"Oh," Sam said curiously. "Well, anyway, so … do you want to?"

Spencer paused. "Guess I haven't thought about it so much."

Sam looked down for a moment. "Sure ya have. You got a boner comin' out of your shorts right now just talkin' about it."

Spencer looked down as well. The night was also too hot for underwear. "OK. Yes."

"Well there ya go. I guess the twelve-year-old was just advanced for his age!"

Silence, then Spencer asked, "Have you ever …."

"You mean …?"

"Yeah."

"Well, no."

"I don't mean just with her. With, um, Charlene there."

Sam paused. "No."

"Have you thought about it?"

"Well, yeah, ya know? I mean, of course I have."

"Got ten dollars?"

"Yeah. I mean, I could get it. What about you?"

Spencer thought of the red sock on the top shelf of his closet. He kept his money in it. "Yeah."

As Spencer was lying back in bed he heard his mother calling quietly from below. "Spencer? Are you up? I thought I heard something." He looked at the clock. How the hell could the time be two thirty? And why was she up?

He did not reply, but pulled the top sheet over him just in case. When she did not call again he was relieved, but his relief was taken when he heard the stairs squeak. She had been on the second or third step, probably, while he came in the window and got back in bed. Maybe she already looked in his room.

He removed the sheet, stared at the ceiling. Twelve? How could that be so? Still, there are boys fourteen, fifteen who seem not to have noticed what's happened between their legs, puberty having never reached their tiddlywinks imaginations, boys who ask their mamas for new underwear and haircuts. Yet elsewhere that bucking twelve-year-old, however mythical, might be beginning to think thoughts he can do nothing about.

In the morning his mother said nothing. He was hoping she'd say something.

Matters of the loins rarely include fully conscious planning, at any stage in life. In the windowless offices of the subconscious, however, schemes are laid out with method, and, step by step, foisted on hapless full consciousness. You bet they are.

So then, after breakfast Spencer walked to the Ploughman's Bank with his sock. "Why, you're Annie Carter's boy, aren't ya?"

"Yes. Ma'am. Um, yes ma'am."

"Well, now, and what can I do for *you*?"

"I'd like to get a ten-dollar bill. A nice one. I have ten dollars in this sock. I mean, coins. And a few ones."

"Oh. Well, I can do that for ya. If you'll just put the money on the counter there I'll count it." Spencer placed the sock before her. "Um, out of the sock, if ya please."

"OH! Sure. But I've counted the money. Three times. It's all there."

"Yes, well, I'm sure it is, but I still have to count it. This is a bank, after all, and I'm responsible for any shortage in my drawer."

After counting Spencer's sock money the teller told, "Why yes, ten dollars to the penny. You must be a real good student, I'll bet!" Spencer smiled a dopey smile. The teller cut the strap on a stack of new tens. "Here ya go young man, a nice, brand new ten dollar bill. Are ya' goin' to buy a toy with it? Maybe a G.I. Joe?" Right then Spencer knew he didn't want a bill so crisp, that somehow crisp money would make him look not so worldly, but he did not want to expand an already awkward transaction. He folded the bill carefully, placing it in his shirt pocket.

From the bank he walked to the alley behind the feed store. Judging by the pattern of windows, two apartments were above the store, accessible by a crooked staircase leading to a faded plank porch. On the right was Charlene's place.

Over the next three days Spencer reconnoitered the scene, noting activity at various times in the day. Men, mostly at night, usually after 9:30 or so, parked at the bottom of the stairs, looked around – some nervously, although some did not look around at all – then went up the stairs, then came back down. Some stayed ten minutes, others half an hour.

Spencer knew what Charlene did was illegal. He figured adults live in a wiggly world, regarding rules, and that authority often seemed to be whatever a grown up man or lady made it at any given time. But, heck, neither she nor her customers made much of an effort to conceal the reality of what was just right there. On the third night he quit trying to make sense of the situation when he saw an off-duty Marvin go up the stairs.

On day four Spencer showered, and brushed his teeth three times. He decided earlier the use of the services of a prostitute by a child required a daytime venue. He thought this less unbecoming, and he didn't want to deal with anyone but Charlene – no men coming out of the night.

At the base of the stairs he checked his pocket for the ten, gave a quick look around, then walked up the wobbly flight. Some children have more fortitude at thirteen (or twelve, if Sam was somehow right) than many people gain across entire lives. Spencer was one. He entered the center door that led to a common hall, wondering if Charlene might confirm the twelve-year-old, removing him from myth. Then he figured that would be a bad idea. He knocked.

"Huh?" was all his knock got him. He tried again. "Yeah, come in." Spencer opened the door and walked in to find Charlene in bed. She conducted business in a one-room apartment. The space had at one time been just a room, someone's office, then was jury-rigged with a galley kitchen into an eight-dollar-a-week flop, bath down the hall. Her place smelled of sprays used to cover up odors.

Expecting to see a daytime john Charlene instead found a lanky boy with a magazine face. She first reacted without words, not only to this Boy Scout but his full-daylight, late-morning call. Then, "Can I help ya, sweetie? Can I direct ya to wherever you're headed?" She laughed, "I mean, this ain't the picture show, ya know."

Spencer continued his assessment. Based on cat houses from cowboy movies, or love nests from 007 exploits, Charlene's digs were a letdown. He was unsure about the age of the woman in the bed, except she really wasn't young, not young young, not anymore. "Are, are you Charlene?"

"Why, yes," Charlene said in some surprise, and then a smile. "Yes I am. Now just why are ya here, sonny?"

Spencer dog-cocked his head. "Don't you know?"

"Well, hon, I guess I don't." Still perky, she said, "Now look, why don't ya just tell Charlene wha—Now wait just a minute! Ya, ya didn't come to…."

"Yes. I did."

Charlene eyed Spencer with suspicion. "Shut the door." Spencer complied. Charlene cocked her own head. "How old are you?"

Spencer knew the slightest pause would speak the truth, and that pause was already in the past. Worse, he stumbled over the beginning of the one-word fib. "F-, fourteen." Worse still he added, "And a half." A slow doubt had started eclipsing his motives with his knock, and now it quickened.

Charlene was silent, looking at him with eyes that

said more than words ever could, looking at him without blinking for quite a number of seconds.

The sheet covering her was printed with small yellow flowers that mocked the dinginess of the fabric. Calling Spencer's bluff she gathered the left side of the sheet with her right hand and in a single motion displayed herself, but keeping her legs together. Spencer's eyes widened in sync with his jaw dropping as he stepped back. "Now you," she instructed, if not demanded.

"Wh-, what?" Spencer now wondered what the hell he was doing here, wondering in stark reality.

"Ya heard me. Drop those shorts and your Sears underwear, Mr. Fourteen-year-old. Oh, and a half."

Spencer was a year from fourteen and that half, of course, and knew what those months would bring, down there-wise. He had spotted a few sapling hairs, but that hint, he figured, was probably not his one-way pass out of early-teen monasticism.

"I, I…. No!" He turned for the door, reaching for the knob clumsily.

Charlene recovered her body. "Stop, kid. Turn around. Please." Spencer did, and now mostly looked at the worn planks of the floor. "Let me tell ya somethin'. You're a smart young man, ya really are. Ya just made one of the best decisions of your life." With her lips she pulled a Newport from a floppy pack, then fingered a kitchen match, making contact with a surface along the way in a graceful arc that ended at the tip of the cigarette. She pulled a drag, waving the match dead, then pushed her lower lip forward to make the exhaled smoke stream upward. "Look, kid, these days … well, I'm best enjoyed with the lights out. Or dim, anyway. If ya know what I mean and I think ya do. Ya know, you are a very handsome boy. In a couple of years you'll have no trouble gettin' fresh meat."

Without expectation, of course, Charlene became enamored with this boy. She admired his spunk and considered inviting him to stay, just to talk, but she knew such an encounter with someone else's child was not possible. "Listen," she began, in a motherly tone that quashed whatever the moment ever was for Spencer. "I shouldn't be your first. You'll want someone who giggles. OK?"

"OK," Spencer said with no hesitation, bobbing his head a bit. He felt embarrassment flush into his face, but instead of turning again for the door he moved towards Charlene, startling her once more.

She saw him pull a new ten from his pocket and place it on the nightstand. "Oh, honey, no, ya don't need to—"

"I want you to have it. I owe you this. You earned it."

"But—"

"And thank you." Spencer did walk to the door now,

turning to look at Charlene. "Goodbye."

Charlene watched the door close, then listened to his precious footsteps fade. She smiled winsomely to herself, for herself. She laughed, just a little, at knowing that on the streets of town still lived a rumor among boys nearing the end of boyhood, a hush that told of a whore with ten dollar tricks.

And so, maybe the truest human emotion is yearning, for she would have taken that beautiful boy in – gladly and eagerly and probably lovingly – without transaction, simply because he was there. She would have done so not out of lust or unspoken perversion, but only and simply to entertain the vampirism the not young can have for the young.

The street rumor was once true. It was no longer true only because the years passed and ten dollars diluted into twenty-five, that's all. Otherwise, she was a once twenty-year-old whim who became, through no effort beyond turning calendar pages, a forty-year-old diversion, along the way never telling sons she once knew their fathers, or even the other way about.

At one time, which didn't seem that long ago, she was going to be....

Charlene reclined fully now, closing her eyes. She held a long pillow on top of her and imagined it to be the beautiful boy. What if she had allowed him to put it in her, not that he would have or could have. Still, had he she might have then imagined the time that didn't seem that long ago, and she could have giggled.

But then Charlene was savvy. Of course she was. For two decades she walked the slim line of winks and nods and whispers among and within the morés of townsfolk. And, come on, there was never a twelve year old. Never.

The town was small enough to make competition moot, and she knew many men came from well beyond town and from the outlying ranches. Charlene's expenses were slim, although she was the first in town to buy a color TV. Still, once in each month she would dress like Sunday and walk to the Ploughman's Bank. Inside she withdrew her deposit box from the vault and an assistant manager would carry it into a little room with a louvered door and she would increase its contents. The box was a larger one that cost her five dollars per month to rent. Inside was a sum in excess of $122,000 cash, yes, for the time when her body expired and twenty-five would start inching back towards ten. For when dim lights wouldn't be dim enough, or maybe for when to get twenty-five she'd have to go three-way, an embarrassment she had always and flatly refused. Even when offered fifty or seventy-five, on at least one occasion a cool c note by that guy from Houston.

The Paris of her mind was Dallas, she always

thought, although her realistic subconscious knew Dallas was far too big now, and so she decided on Austin. She'd buy a nice house, small but not too. A yard. Maybe a dog, maybe one of those Boston terriers she'd name Ted Dog. She'd never owned a car, never really needed one given the radius of her life, but maybe she'd buy a Mustang, like the one Mary Tyler Moore drove into Minneapolis every Saturday night.

And so, she took satisfaction in not allowing what might have been. She knew she could have encouraged the boy, grabbed him playfully. Pulling him to her, pulling the shorts off his skinny butt, taking his smoothness into her mouth.

Anyway, she knew he would cry – she'd watched seventeen-year-old quarterbacks who looked almost twenty break down – and yank his shorts on in shame and the snot of his stumble, stuffing his underpants into a pocket. And she would have already sunk her fangs into his neck, pulling in his blood, or any stuff of youth, pushing him to a tangent he was, ten minutes earlier, never to have known.

She considered still the time that didn't seem all that long ago, it really didn't, and tried remembering the path she had been shoved from half her lifetime back, when she still might have become what she was going to be.

The Situation Without a Choice That Involved Jack at Twelve

The problem was whenever Harriet drove a car she gave the task the same level of attention required to soak in a hot tub. If she wasn't actively smoking a cigarette she was lighting the next one while shifting gears. The geezer rock station she favored was listened to at about 8.5 out of ten. "All right, man, 'Layla.' Yes!" In the back seat was a rock pile of crumpled Wendy's bags, so while doing all the aforementioned activities she could simultaneously chow down a cheeseburger, fries and a Coke. This circus could have been worse had she cared for Frosties. She wore her unbuckled seat belt over her left shoulder. "Give a cop what he wants to see, I always say."

The overall risk assessment of her decades-old driving habits had been notched up in recent years by talking on the phone. Now wrap this entire package in the fact Harriet had not been completely sober, in a literal quantitative way, for any minute of any given day since somewhere in 1971. Not regarding C_2H_5OH, THC or, for that matter, Bubba's BBQ and hash browns and hash brownies. Her state had been continuously altered since Nixon. Well, this is how Carol saw the deal anyway, about her sister.

Carol was the flip side of Harriet – the negation or inversion or simply reflexive opposite of her sib. She had been kicked out of nun school for being over pious. OK, not really. Still, though. Yep, sometimes kids in families go north and south on parents. Nature, nurture, genes, whatever. Hell, just ask Lillian Carter – Jimmy, Billy, whatever.

Carol, of course, had not heard "Layla" approximately six thousand, eight hundred sixty-four times, based on three times per week for the last two thousand, two hundred eighty-eight weeks. She had also not heard "Stairway…" or "Satisfaction" or "A Day in the Life" by the thousands of listens either. Or "Old Man" or "We got the Beat" or "Light my Fire."

"All right, man, 'Roundabout.' Yes!"

The overriding problem of Harriet would be magnified in an ancillary way by sort of an approaching grand conjunction of extended family. Actually, a non-grand conjunction based on who wasn't in place when Carol needed them to be, the phenomenon of absences aligning into a perfect procession of holes. Carol would reach a point one afternoon at which who was available became eleven or twelve holes, then Harriet. ("Let me ask you something," was Harriet's extant question, asked at least twice a week to most anyone. "What kind of God damned name is *Harriet*? Hell, why didn't they just name me Gertrude, for God's sake. Or Matilda. Can you imag—All right, man, 'Tangled Up in Blues.' Hell yes!")

Harriet's go-to defense, regarding her driving, was simply, "Hey! I never have an open container." More to the point, her driving record, which no one, including Harriet, talked about but everyone knew about. As these situations go once in a while, Harriet had never had a DUI, she had never been in an accident, had never gotten a ticket. In point of fact, counselor, she had never even been pulled over, not once, not even for something as innocent as expired tags or the proverbial burned-out taillight leading to a bust. She had always been like a kitten crossing eight lanes of traffic without a ding.

In just the past six months Carol had been ticketed twice for speeding. Rolling through a stop sign, three ordinary parking tickets and one each for parking in a fire lane and in an ambulance zone. And, of course, expired tags. Over the years she had been in three at-fault accidents, including T-boning a carload of nuns, and this time no kidding.

Kettle. Black. Perception. Reality. Yeah.

OK. Carol's daughter Natalie was even squarer than her mom. Like, man, a cube. Her son, Jack, was swimming one afternoon at one of those McMansions with gabled gables and columns all over inside and TV screens so big just one wouldn't fit in a VW Microbus. Enough square footage to get lost in on an acre lot surrounded by other acre lots holding more great-roomed and rear-staired Barbie Castles, all these lots way the hell out somewhere, beyond the Golden Wings mega church, pastures of patio villas – Wooded Glen, Glenwood Woods and Vista View Harbour – and the abandoned Wal-Mart just down the road from the new Super Wal-Mart.

Carol was looking after Jack, a good kid, while Natalie and her husband Troy were away at a couples' retreat, trying earnestly to save their marriage through Jesus. The marriage, in point of fact, needed saving mightily, so, heck, might as well give Jesus a crack at it. Carol was to pick Jack up at exactly 4:30. "Don't be late," Natalie told her mother, "Marie Ann becomes very annoyed when anyone is late. *Very* annoyed."

Carol did not want to jeopardize Natalie's friendship with Marie Ann, who drove a Range Rover and had a separate closet for shoes, including a small gaggle of those Italian jobs that run two grand a pair, as in ten Benjamin's per foot, or four Grants per toe. "And for God's sake don't call her Ann Marie," Natalie reminded and warned her mother. Carol had, in fact, called Marie Ann Ann Marie more than a few times in conversation with her daughter, and once or twice to Marie Ann's face. She was already on thin ice with Ann Ma—er, Marie Ann.

At 3:50 Carol received a call, wouldn't you know, from her neighbor Sally who called Carol after calling 911 and after tending to the situation with Larry, Carol's husband.

Larry been teetering on the top rung of his sixteen-foot extension ladder in pursuit of a small sycamore branch stuck in a gutter. He would have been OK had he not reached for the branch, extending his left arm fully while raising his right foot, thus moving the center of mass in the overall system well beyond the vertical. But he did reach. The ladder fell from under him to the left and clanged on the ground as Larry grabbed the gutter with both hands and hung there for a bit like the Warner Brothers' Coyote. Meep meep. The guttering began pulling away as Larry was losing his grip. He and twenty feet of guttering came down on top of the taxus bushes. There's little need for specifics at this point, simply that Larry was, in a word, broken. Carol needed to get to the hospital as soon as she could, but first she had to deal with Marie Ann not becoming annoyed. *Very* annoyed.

She started calling. Her other sister. Their brother. Her sister-in-law. Her neighbor. Her other neighbor. Her mall-walking partner. Her other neighbor's babysitter. And so on and so forth, etcetera. Eventually calling even her cleaning lady. Some of those calls went right to voice mail, which meant their phones weren't even turned on. Of those who did answer, no one could help her, they'd like to but they just really couldn't, not just now, thanks for calling, have a good the rest of your afternoon.

As the human mind works, of course, Harriet had begun peering up from Carol's subconscious since about halfway through her unresponsive calling spree. Carol had poked around in dusty corners of her memory trying to think of someone, almost anyone – what's the name of that man with one arm? – who could help her, all while Harriet's impersonation of Cheech and/or Chong became clearer and closer to the conscious surface. Closer, closer … POP! Hello!

"Oh, no. I just can't," Carol said aloud and to no one. "I cannot send Harriet to pick up Jack, not at Marie Ann's." *What will she think about Natalie after meeting Harriet? Marie Ann is the only one Natalie knows with a shoe closet, after all.* But Carol was now in a situation without a choice. The time was 4:12. *Don't be late* tick tick tick *Marie Ann becomes very annoyed when anyone is late* tock tock tock.

Shoe closet. Built-in Sub-Zero. Wine cellar. Rover.

Carol did have both of Harriet's numbers, in case something happened and she had to get in touch with Harriet. And now something had happened. But it wasn't something that had happened requiring only that

Harriet be informed, no, not simply a dead second cousin or, more casually, even, oh, tornadic destruction of a childhood landmark. No, this something at hand was a relationship sort of two-way deal that was happening now. Right now. Yikes.

"Harriet? It's Carol. Look, I—"

"Yeah? Carol my sister?"

"Well, yes, Harriet, your *sister*. Now please listen, I—"

"What's wrong? Who died? I'm asking, you know, because that's the only reason you'd ever—All right, man. Joe Cocker. Yes!"

"Harriet there *is* something wrong and I need your help. Larry is in the hospital. He—"

"Larry?"

"My husband, Harriet."

"Oh yeah. The dentist."

"He's an orthodontist."

"Yeah. Teeth."

"Harriet! Please listen to me. I—"

"Why's he in the hospital?"

"He fell off a ladder. Now look I need your help. I need you to pick up Jack – YOUR NEPHEW – at a house in Buckingham Estates."

"Where?"

"Buckingham Estates. It's out Lincoln Road, beyond the freeway loop."

"Way out there?"

"It's really not that far, Harriet, and I really need your help. Can you leave now? It's important that Jack be picked up as soon as possible."

"Oh. Well, like, for real?"

"Yes, Harriet, for real."

"Oh. Well, sure, Carol. If I can help, damn, I'm on it!"

"Really?"

"Sure. Hey, why are we here, man, if we can't help each other, you know?"

"Uh, yes. Well, I'm so glad you feel that way. Now, the address is 5103 Charrington Cross Way. You'll go out—"

"Wait, wait, just let me write it down, that's all. I've got a stick-on GPS now. Freddie gave it to me."

There was no time to ask who Freddie is, or was. "OK. It's 5-1-oh-3 Charrington Cross Way. Got it?"

"Yep, got it."

"So you're on your way?"

"Not as long as I'm talkin' to you."

Then, "Hello, Ann Mar—Marie Ann? This is Carol! Natalie's mother. I'm calling because something has happened and I can't pick up Jack, and the person who will won't be there until about 5:00. I'm terribly sorry but my hus—"

"Late?" Marie Ann said. "LATE?"

"Well, yes. You see my hus—"

"I run a tight schedule, Carol. If your grandchild is picked up late I'LL be late for my Pilates. In fact, so late I might as well not go. So this just won't do."

"Yes, yes I understand. But this is an emer—"

"I'm to meet my husband for dinner. We have reservations for Chez Fromage at 7:30."

"Well I'm *very* sorry, but, well, can't you go anyway and leave Jack with Elliot?"

"I'm not leaving two boys alone, Carol. Don't you watch the news?"

"They're twelve years old. It's only for thirty minutes."

"Exactly my point, Carol. Twelve."

"Well, my husband has been severely injured. Surely you can understand my situation. Marie Ann."

A very long pause followed, but Carol held her ground. Finally Marie Ann said, "All right. All right! Apparently my Pilates will have to wait. We agreed on 4:30. We did! But then some people.... OK, all right, who will be picking Jack up, picking him up at five. FIVE! Thirty-eight minutes from now." Tick tock.

"My sister Harriet. Jack's great aunt."

"What kind of car does she have, so I'll know when she arrives? At five."

"Well, a, it's a—"

"A what?"

"It's a, an Oldsmobile. Kind of a purple-ish red."

"*Olds*mobile? Those aren't even made anymore, are they?"

"Well, I guess not."

"All right, Carol. I'll make this sacrifice. Five o'clock, right?"

"Oh yes! Harriet will be there at five. You can count on it! And if there's any problem—"

"Why should there be any problems? She'll be here, won't she? At five. F-i-v-e."

"Yes, yes. I mean should you have a question my cell number is—"

"It's on my screen. This *is* the twenty-first century, Carol."

"Yes. Well thank you so much A—Marie Ann," Carol said, wondering if she could really count on diddly-squat from Harriet. She felt an urge to call Harriet on her cell to make sure she was moving right along, but stopped herself. But then she did call Harriet's landline. Ring ring ring ring click. "Howdy, pardner, Kiki's not at the ranch right now, so leave a smoke signal and I'll beam some thoughts back your way later. See ya!" Oh dear, oh dear oh dear oh dear. *Kiki? What? KIKI? Who on Earth is Kiki?* Anyhoo, Carol figured Harriet had left, and that was good, and what she had done was all she could do.

Carol had been at the hospital for about twenty minutes, consoling a now conscious Larry, talking with doctors, going over insurance with an admitting clerk. Her phone rang and she wondered who on Earth it could be and she glanced down and it was Marie Ann and she said to the clerk, "I'm sorry, but I must take this call, it concerns my grandson."

"Carol, this is Marie Ann. Some kind of burned-out hippie claiming to be your sister is here. I'm double checking your arrangements before I release Jack."

"Yes, um, yes. That's Harriet. She's picking him up. It's, it's all right." Carol looked at her watch to find 4:58. Bingo! At least she had two minutes of respectability on deposit at the Bank of Marie Ann.

"I see. Well as you can understand, I suppose, I was reluctant to turn over someone else's child to Janis Joplin here."

What? How the heck does someone from the Michael Bolton years even know about Janis? "He can go with her. She's his aunt. His great-aunt. Great-aunt Harriet, so it's OK. And it's five o'clock."

Fortunately Jack, at twelve, was eager to start breaking free from his Pottery Barn for Kids life (especially having learned recently of PB teens). However anomalously in present day, he was looking for life without apps. What had emerged in the last few minutes seemed astonishingly app free and he stepped in seamlessly.

"Hello, Aunt Harriet. It's good to see you again."

"I thought she's your great-aunt. That's what your grandmother said."

"Well, she is, but that's a lot to say. Kind of awkward. Well, good-bye Elliot. Thank you for inviting me. Good-bye, Mrs. Williams." With that Jack started moving for the door. Harriet followed quickly.

"Hey, yeah good-bye," Harriet waved. "Thanks for your understanding and, like, you know." As they walked to her car she could feel Marie Ann's gaze from a dining room window drilling into her. "Hey, thanks for your help back there. That was some performance, um…."

"Jack."

"Yeah. Jack."

Jack said in a rip-off British accent, "And you must be my great-aunt Harriet."

"Hell yeah. Whatever, man. So you know about your granddad? He fell off a roof."

"Mrs. Williams just said he'd been hurt. Is he OK?"

"Well, I don't think so, but I guess he's OK enough, or we would have heard. So, look, I think we'd better get out of here." She started the engine, the radio came on. "All right, man, 'Get Down on Me.' Yes!" Harriet put the gear selector in reverse.

"You have a stick shift?"

"Sure, Jack. It's the only way to fly. Only weenies

drive automatics."

"Yeah. On my Dad's car there's just a dial. He just dials the gears, like opening a jar of mayonnaise."

"Yeah, well, tell me about it. This is an Oldsmobile Achieva. Kind of a dorky car, but I like it. It's got a five-speed Getrag hooked up to 3.3 V-6. I mean, it's nothin' like—All right, man 'Fire and Rain.' Yes!"

"Like what?"

"What?"

"It's nothing like what?"

"Oh, yeah. I mean, this little ride is OK. I mean, it's not like I'm drivin' around in some rice burner. You know, man, a Kia or whatever. But it's nothin' like the '69 GTO I had back in the day. Dark green over black, convertible. It—"

"CONVERTIBLE? My mom has a sunroof she's never opened."

"Yeah, man. It was beautiful. Bought it in '72 from a good friend. It had a four speed hooked up to a freakin' 455. That's cubic inches, pal, back then, so that's like a freakin' seven-and-change-liter powerhouse today."

"Awesome!"

"Yeah! That's some house back there. So that Elliot is your friend?"

"He's more like the son of my Mom's friend, I guess."

"Oh. Yeah? Hmm. So, you like cars?"

"I kind of like old cars. I read that cars forty or fifty years ago weren't full of computers. I kind of like that idea, Aunt Harriet."

"OK, look, we're gonna to need to stop the aunt thing."

"OK. Harriet," Jack said, giving her a sideways.

"Yeah, and we're gonna have to stop that, too. My friends call me Kiki."

"Yeah?"

"Yeah."

"For how long?"

"Well, maybe forty years."

"I've never heard anyone call you that."

"Guess that shows how close we are as sisters, your mother and me. And, well, whoever else."

"I guess that's true. Could I ask you something, Kiki? Would you mind?"

"Well, I don't know. What is it?"

"Well, it's just that … my mom said you did a lot of drugs. Or that you still do."

"Oh yeah?"

"Yeah. She did."

"Well, you know, I kind of think your mom hasn't updated her files on me in a long time. But, yeah, I'm not gonna lie. I once did a lot of drugs. I still smoke some weed, but not as much as your mom and grandma think."

"But that's illegal."

"Yeah, it is. But then, an awful lot of crappy stuff *is* legal. I mean, I'm not tryin' to weasel out of anything, legal-wise, I'm just answerin' your question. Straightforward. Your grandma must be in a real pickle, to have called me. I know I was her last hope, to pick you up from la-la land out there. She probably thinks I'm not firing on all cylinders right now."

"Well, I was just curious. I'm not judging you."

"That's good. Thank you."

They drove on a bit. "There's a boy in my neighborhood I know. He's fourteen, I think. His deal is being *off* drugs. Isn't that funny? Sometimes he doesn't take his Ritalin, because he wants to remember what it was like when he was normal."

"Well there you go, the whole deal backwards, then."

"Yeah. Why did you do drugs?"

"Jack, pal, you know everybody does drugs, even when they're not chemicals. Goin' to church, watchin' *Star Trek,* whatever. Everybody has a happy place, and they want a way to get there."

For a while Jack looked out his window again as they moved along. "I was wondering, Kiki, did you, well, take LSD? I read on Wikipedia it used to be legal."

"Yeah, that's right. The Army conducted experiments on volunteers."

"The Army?"

"Yep. They were interested in drug warfare, pharma-co … well, whatever. In the early '60s. I did it once, around '74. It wasn't so great an experience. Actually, it was bad. I figured out real soon after my mind expanded into some weird places. Places best left unvisited. Places of the id."

"The id?"

"The id. That's the part of the brain that makes mental sausage. Best not to see how it's done. For me, anyway."

"I'm not sure I get it."

"Good."

They drove on a bit more. "Do you think we should go by the hospital?"

"Your grandma said to take you home, straight home. So I guess that's the best thing. I guess it's pretty hectic at the hospital."

But then they stopped at Wendy's, so Great Aunt Harriet could at least buy her great nephew a cheese-burger. "Guess I owe you a lot of Christmas presents, Jack."

"OK. But I guess I owe you some, too."

As they drove along Bayshire Drive Harriet said, "Let me know which one it is."

"It's three up on the left. You've never been here?"

"I think they've been here just a couple of years, so I've never made it over."

"I guess they'll be at the hospital for a while."

"Yep. I guess your grandma will be there 'til midnight, maybe."

"It's right here, Kiki."

They pulled into the driveway. "I hope everything works out as well. I'll be thinkin' about your granddad. It was good to see you again, Jack."

"Yeah." Jack sat pivoted on the seat, his feet now on the pavement. Then, "Look, I … I'm afraid I don't remember you much. Not really."

"Well, you wouldn't. It's been a while. You were little."

"Midnight, huh?"

"Probably."

"Kiki, would you like to come in? Please?"

Kiki thought for a moment. She looked around at the well-kept houses, all with a little too much throwback charm. Towheaded kids on weedless lawns. Maybe Thomas Kincade with his easel set up somewhere. "Why not, Jack. Hell yes."

Boy in Shadow

They lived in a wide river valley that would produce overcast days, without rain but preserving existing moisture from previous rainy days. On those days the boy might appear. He would not appear in direct sunlight, or on hotter days, days with an air temperature above eighty degrees or so.

Their house sat near the end of a road to nowhere, off another road to nowhere. Big houses on rolling lots that reflected the effortless optimism of white people in the middle of the century that was America's century. Mostly the usual columned colonials and some Tudors, but then also a few rambling glass-walled houses, a California incursion that once crossed the Mississippi into parochial burgs and towns as Sputnik orbited above. However, theirs was a home of collected adorned boxes and wainscoting and quoins, and rather ridiculous Corinthian columns. They had neighbors, but with one hundred or more feet between houses the notion of next door was loose.

And even so, the particulars of the shape and terrain

of their lot, and how the lot itself was situated along the lane, gave a further curtain of privacy. Not hard to find really, just easy to miss.

Their sloped yard provided for a walk-out lower level. At the bottom property divide stood dense woods beyond a creek after half an acre of open lawn.

At the divide the woods began a climb up to another ridge, which peaked at about the same level as their second floor. She did not know who owned the property beyond the creek, and its trees, some of which were oaks a big man could not hug and touch his fingertips. Hemlocks seventy-five feet high. Although she knew they were not, the woods looked primeval. On those humid overcast days loose cotton balls of mist hung in the canopy. She had never entered the woods, not once in twenty-two years.

From these woods the boy emerged. Across two summers the boy would come just four times. But four times would be enough.

Over the past many years she became a private person, reticent to engage, sometimes awkward when engaged. On the first visit, when she saw the boy emerge from the woods and begin his climb up their back lawn, she was perturbed and felt invaded. "You there," she shouted down the slope, "what are you doing here? This is a private yard." But he proceeded without pause.

He might have been thirteen or fourteen – he would never say – but she figured he was more likely twelve. Although he didn't so much have a child's high voice, she could tell his voice had not changed. Still, his fingers were slender and long, having outgrown any pudgy and dimpled hands of a single-digit boy age. He was well built and a notch above five feet. He sported a sort of haphazard handsomeness.

"I wonder if I might have some water?" he asked brightly. "It's warming up." He looked above. "The clouds are thinning."

"Where did you come from?" She nearly demanded. "Where are you going?"

He answered her first question by pointing to the woods. The answer to her second question was completely obvious.

"Come sit down, then. Right here" she instructed, pointing to a webbed chair. "I'll get your water."

In the lower level living area was a bar with a small sink. As she filled a glass she watched this boy through a window as he surveyed the sky.

Handing the boy his water she relaxed her tone. "What's your name? I'm Mrs. Adams. Barbara Adams."

His delay in answering spanned not one second, yet

it was long enough to suggest he used the time to invent. "Walter."

"Walter? That's not a usual name, not these days."

"No, it isn't," the boy agreed. "This is very good water. Thank you."

"You're very welcome. Walter. Do you live around here? Across the ridge?"

Again just the flash of a delay. "Yes."

During the conversation the clouds continued to weaken. The boy squinted, then, looking back down, spread the fingers of his left hand, watching the projection on the bricks of the terrace. She heard him whisper to himself, "Shadow."

"Walter, would you like some more water? Maybe some lemonade?"

"No. But thank you, Mrs. Adams." He scanned the sky again. "I have to go now."

"But—" was all she could say before the boy turned to head back downhill. Her back yard faced west and the late afternoon shadows from the woods were now a quarter way up the slope. She watched as he ran to the terminator of the sunline. Once across he slowed to a walk. A few steps later he stopped for a few seconds, then turned and gave a wave that was simply raising his right hand, without further motion. He grinned, but that sentiment was not much carried into his eyes.

She continued to watch him descend, cross the creek

and then move into the woods. She focused to spot him within the trees, but soon could not. A few minutes later she wasn't fully convinced he had been at all, until she saw the glass. A glass of water half full and a few words were the evidence of his visit.

She took the glass and put it aside, unwashed, under the bar.

Money buys ease and convenience, of course. In many cases, for better or worse, money in excess also buys insulation from the world of less easy lives. The real lives, or very different ones, anyway. She had been insulated her entire life, her husband only somewhat less so. Roger enjoyed the business world, which was in fact sport to him. He had been good at getting ahead and was presently good at keeping ahead. Hence, even with every want and whim delivered bank balances overflowed.

No amount of financial brimming changed her inner circumstances, though. She had a number of acquaintances. She had maybe a few friends, but she felt she always needed to re-spark friendship whenever she called someone, considering few ever called her. Roger and she knew other couples, but only as a result of Roger's business intersections. There was barely enough work for the cleaning lady to come two days a week, but she added a third simply to have another person in the house. The two often played cards and would sometimes go to lunch. Even, a time or two, at the club.

That evening held a dinner engagement with one of Roger's business associates. With a start she realized the time, 5:30, and became aware she had done nothing to ready herself. She would not mention Walter to Roger, and within a day or two mostly forgot about the strange boy.

Mostly.

But, well then, the subconscious mind is where ideas and anticipations and yearnings emerge – from star stuff that is presently our brains – into full consciousness.

You bet it is. And so while Walter's visit faded a little each day in her conscious mind, below decks grew an anticipation of a second visit that tickled awareness in the fully conscious mind and suggested the presently unclaimed prize of a real Walter.

Real. Real?

The next morning she asked her husband, "Roger, do you know what lies over the ridge, behind our property? Are any houses there? Some kind of settlement?"

"A settlement? That's an odd thought. Well, no, there are no houses. Just a few ramshackle barns, and I guess what's left of a farmhouse. That's the old Richmond place, eight hundred acres. The land remains in the family. They won't sell. Eight hundred acres of woods and pasture. Prime real estate. In fact the property starts just on the other side of our creek."

On a day after the first visit Barbara put on her gardening shoes, but not those clothes. She walked down the hill, stopping before the creek. She scanned the woods at many levels and found herself thinking mightily about Walter. Perhaps she might transmit some sort of signal, alerting Walter, causing him to come. Perhaps. But, well of course such a notion was ridiculous. Did she expect antennae to rise from her head?

So then children who are just barely so, or maybe no longer so, if only by maybe a season, or by a hormone just released, can be compelling, magnetic. Captivating. Some are doltish young wags unrecognizing of what lies ahead and of certain possibilities along that future path. Boys now deep voiced who, when alone, pull their old train sets from dusty cardboard boxes in hall closets and make chocolate milk in the kitchen.

Walter was not one of these backwards-looking boys, she considered, to the extent of giving the scent of a human who already knew the full run of the days of a life. Or knew of them, at any rate. Oh, what a curious boy!

The woods, just right there across the creek, were so

a place in which she was not. Borderless and swimming in a give and take of life. Time slipped and at first she did not hear Roger approaching, calling her name. She looked at her watch and gasped slightly before spouting, "Roger!"

"What are you doing way down here? Looking for someone?"

"Oh, well, no. Not at all. I was just, oh, I don't know, just looking over at that Richmond place."

"I don't think you've been down here, to the creek," Roger began, quickly regretting this start, "I mean, well, since…."

No, she hadn't been down to the creek since Bradley. She did not finish the sentence her husband left hanging. "Oh, I don't know, Roger, I…. You know, it's really another world over there, just beyond. It really is."

"Yes, I suppose it is. Are … are you all right then, Barbara?

"Yes, Roger. I'm fine. It's just that—"
"Yes?"

She could not tell him about Walter even as she was ready to. No. No. "It's really nothing. I thought I might see some interesting birds. That's all."

Roger considered his wife with smiling affection. He turned to face the house and offered his right hand. She returned his smile, grasped his fingers into her own and they climbed the hill together.

When August was almost finished she knew Walter was indeed real – had been real – when she looked out the bow window of the dining room to see him standing on the terrace. She tapped on a pane. Walter looked up smiling, and found her own smile in place. She opened a door to the upper terrace to make her way quickly down the spiral staircase of wrought iron.

The boy's clothes were casual on that first visit, really the bare minimum of the dressed human animal, outside of the pool, and now he wore the same clothes again, a white T-shirt with red hems on the sleeves and neck, light tan shorts and simple white sneakers without socks. The clothes were clean, although threadbare along seams here and there. As he sat she noticed his paleness, no tan lines where clothes and bare skin met. A strange child of summer, to be given by the solstice; perhaps to be taken by the equinox? She would not realize until late September, when the weatherman mentioned the equinox, that his first visit had been on the solstice day.

Standing on the last step of the staircase she almost yelled, "Walter!" Walter waved back. Her subconscious mind then became insistent. "It's so *good* to see you again!"

"I'm glad to see you again, Mrs. Adams."

She cocked her head a little. "Walter, please call me Barbara."

"Are you sure?" Walter smiled, asking almost rhetorically.

"Yes. Of course. Let me get you some water." She almost asked him to come in, but noticed the heavy clouds and so felt she shouldn't, or that he wouldn't.

"Thank you."

"Or maybe lemonade."

"Yes. That would be nice."

As she filled his glass she looked at Walter through the windows, half expecting him to fade into air. "Here you go, Walter," she said, extending the cold glass. "So, I suppose school will start soon."

"Yes. Probably. I mean, of course. Sure."

"Well, will you start the seventh grade? Or maybe the eighth."

"Well, I guess the eighth. I'm home schooled. Things aren't that exact."

"Oh, I see. How interesting. Does your mother teach you?"

"Sometimes. Do you have children?" he asked, turning to look at her directly.

She paused. "We, well you see we had a son. He died, though."

"When he was about my age?"

Barbara lowered her brows and lost her smile. "As a matter of fact, yes. But, really now, I—"

"I'm sorry. That was rude of me. I mean, insensitive. I didn't mean to ...well ... I mean, I'm sorry to hear that. Very sorry."

"Thank you. It's forgotten."

"So…this is a beautiful house."

"Thank you."

"Have you lived here a long time?"

"Oh, more than twenty years. What is your house like, Walter?"

"Oh, nothing like this."

"Well, is it a one story? A cottage? Is it over the ridge?"

Walter looked away. "I need to be going."

"But—Oh, I see. Well then, will you be back?"

"Oh yes. Goodbye." Walter stood, turned and began his return. He stopped and turned again. "Mrs. Ad—, um, Barbara? What was his name?"

For a moment she did not understand. But then she said, "Bradley."

"Bradley," Walter repeated.

"Yes. That's right."

Walter turned again and walked away. He did not see her knees give way as she buckled into a webbed chair, and he did not hear her weep.

After the second visit she removed Walter's water glass from his first, from under the bar a time or two, to simply look at it and hold it. In September she took out the water glass almost every day. One day she drank from it, from all around the rim so her lips would be where his had been. By the end of September, beyond the equinox now, Walter had not returned. She hoped he might, and then so very much hoped he might even as she understood the tacit bounds of this summer child. She thought about the twenty-two years of keeping to her side of the creek.

A nephew left behind clothing after a visit once, and she figured she was about the size of an older teenaged boy. The hiking shoes fit well and the jeans well enough. This expeditionary getup was completely unlike her and would have shocked her husband, but she was now compelled to enter the woods. If he would not come to her, then she would find him, the season notwithstanding.

She walked down the slope of their back lawn with a slowing pace. She halted at the edge, the creek providing the divide. Another step would take her into terra incognito, a land of shadow even with the sun full above.

Bradley and she, when he was eight, nine, would play down here. Sometimes they would pitch a tent – he would say *Let's play camper* – and have their lunch and tie strings to small fallen branches and pretend to fish. Standing at the creek's edge she remembered she had never let her son cross into the woods. With a start she recalled a motherly something from those days, reflexive, like placing her arm in front of her child in the car during a sudden stop.

But then she did indeed make her way with one step, then another. The creek was shallow and she saw rocks scattered regularly enough to make steppingstones and smiled as she thought Walter must use this same elevated rock path. The light was dappled, of course, under the canopy, but also reduced as the zenith of the sun became a bit lower with each day, as the northern hemisphere now tilted away from the sun. She noticed a clump of Dutchman's britches, another of bloodroot. She thought the air temperature was less than it should be, even allowing for the coolness of a forest floor. A motion in her left periphery unfolded into a corn snake slithering across a large smooth stone.

She felt being watched, even as a full turn confirmed her solitude. But only from human eyes, of course. Of course she was being watched, not only by unseen animals, but perhaps by the forest itself. She figured to hike to the ridge to take in the prospect from the top.

About halfway up the hill that was across the creek from her own downward property she stopped. Stopped cold, actually. When later she would think back on the end of her ascent she would wonder if she stopped, or had been stopped. The feeling was not so much of not belonging, but that concessions would be required to go on, as if a polarity shift would now be asked of her in order to gain knowledge of this place immediate.

Before this halt she continued simply putting one foot in front of the other up the slope. But when a time came for her right foot to cycle in she planted it, stopped for not one second, then pivoted around on her left foot and headed for her own property. Her descent was quick without running; deliberate and with purpose.

She would cross the creek to go up the wooded hill once more.

Across fall and winter and the next spring she thought about Walter. When snow was a foot deep down the slope she imagined him making tracks up the hill in boots and a hooded coat and a scarf across his mouth. But then he was not a winter child, of course not. Still, what did he do in winter? Or, simply, where was he? The winter sun could be brighter than the summer sun, doubly so when reflected off the white pack. There was no sharper shadow than a winter shadow, yes, but then no clouds like snow clouds. Was his concern the sunlight, or maybe just the actual heat of summer made more so by direct rays?

For years now at Christmas having a tree was in the same category as having the lawn mowed. Her decorator saw to the chore. Had a tree been her decision she wouldn't have bothered in recent times, yet the tree and many other decorations were needed for the holiday entertaining of Roger's business associates and connections, or a few neighbors on one or another yuletide Thursday night or Sunday afternoon.

But this year she asked Roger to go with her, downtown to the hay market. She wanted a real tree she could decorate herself, as carefully as Bradley and she had once done. Roger balked, then suggested having a tree delivered. "No, Roger. I want a tree tied to the roof of my car. And I want to drive home that way. And decorate it with all our old ornaments. I know where they are in the attic. Loraine can help me."

Roger remembered she had lost interest in decorating the Christmas after Bradley. Then he said, "Certainly. And I'll tell you what. We'll have dinner at Lorenzo's on the way back, tree on top and all!"

That next spring bloomed early, and seemed to insist that summer advance too, but the calendar and the day of solstice stayed put, of course. With a start one day in May, and a stopping of her step, she felt a yearning for the boy. She had been with him a total of one hour, if that, yet he seemed to hold a puzzle piece she didn't know was missing.

On June first in that second year she was sitting in Bradley's room, which was, from the rear view, the double set of windows in the middle, upstairs. She started coming into the room – breaching the threshold, really – soon after last year's equinox.

Bradley would be twenty-three now. Today. After the funeral, on that afternoon, Roger climbed the back stairs and walked to his son's room. He peered in, but did not enter. After just a few minutes he closed the door. Across a decade now the boy's room had been undisturbed. Underwear and socks still in the top dresser drawer. Shoes kicked off and askew where they landed as a pair. Schoolbooks from his final day open on his desk, sheets of homework arrayed among the books, never to be finished. His notion of hanging up clothes and arranging his closet was simply shutting that door, and still now behind that door was piled boyhood entropy.

Twice in each year Barbara would open the door to look in. Christmas. His birthday. In some years she'd open the door a third or fourth time, random days of emptiness in which amplifying the pain seemed to help. But she never stepped in, never crossed that literal threshold. Today held that breach.

Sitting on her son's bed she looked across at the ridge top, questions tumbling through her mind. These questions were not analytical, emerging from the opposite direction, wholly visceral in origin, but over days and weeks and months now had coalesced into the realm of rationality, or as rational as such questions could be. Was Walter from the past, or maybe the future?

Was he Jesus?

Was he Death?

Was he both?

And yet, given their inherent quandaries, she considered these questions only briefly, just bumping into them long enough to bump away. They seemed unanswerable, after all. Still, if they were maybe she was afraid of the answers.

Two days after the next solstice she was walking down the left side of the house. At the bottom, turning the corner, she saw Walter sitting in a terrace chair. "Why, hello Walter."

Walter turned his head. "Oh. Barbara." He stood up to face her in greeting.

"How have you been, Walter?" She looked up at the clouds, which had been gathering since dawn, and now darkened this mid-afternoon. "I'd say this is your kind of day."

"Yes," he beamed.

"I hope you can stay a little longer, this time."

"Oh, I think I can." Walter looked down at his splayed his fingers. No shadow, and none to come. "About our last visit, my questions, your son. Again, I'm sorry."

"Yes, well, please, as I said it's forgotten. So, we'll forget it. OK? Would you like something to eat? I could make us lunch."

"Oh, I don't eat much."

"Well, you must eat something once in a while. I have turkey. Some very good apples. And chili. It's delicious. My husband makes it."

Walter asked with a slight surprise, "Your husband?"

"Yes, my husband. Well, I am married, you know."

"Oh. Yes. Sure. Is his name Bra—. I mean, I guess I don't know his name."

"It's Mr. Adams," she delivered.

"Oh. Sure. Of course."

"Yes, well, then…. You know, I'd like to know something about you. You know quite a bit about me, after all."

"Oh, I'm just a kid."

"Who comes from the woods. Is that right?"

"Yes!"

"Well do you have a brother or a sister?"

"There are a lot of us."

"A lot of who?"

"Us, that's all."

"I see. You know, my husband tells me there's nothing over the ridge but a few old barns and a ramshackle farmhouse. Do you live in the farmhouse?"

Walter looked at her, smiled at her. Despite the

heavy cloud cover and the blocked sun his eyes twinkled. "You're very pretty, Barbara."

She was now outdone with his cheekiness, but could not challenge it, or even respond. His words also twinkled and she simply could not reject them, another puzzle piece she found she needed. Wanted, in fact had hoped for. Finally she got out, "Yes, well, thank you, Walter. But young boys do not say such things to older women."

"No," he considered as no boy should, as no boy could if he weren't …. "No, I suppose they don't," he agreed again as she seemed to wait for an apology. "You know, I was wondering, do you go into the woods?"

A slight hesitation now blurred her own true answer. "No. I looked at them one day. Into them. From across the creek."

"Oh?"

How could he know? Had he been watching? "But … I didn't go in. I didn't go over, I didn't cross the creek." *I was driven from there, told to leave. Do you know that?*

Now Walter surveyed the low sky. "Are you afraid?"

"Afraid? Why, no. The woods are really just not my kind of place, that's all. I mean, I find … well they're…."

"Because there's nothing to fear."

"Well, no. Why should there be?"

"There shouldn't. And there isn't. I could show you."

Barbara felt rescuing rain drops. "I think we'd better

go inside."

"Why?"

"Well, it's raining, you know."

"I love the rain!" Walter beamed.

Barbara thought about the fifty dollars she'd spent on her hair that morning and moved to stand under the upper terrace. The rain was very soon falling hard enough for drops to produce a visible upward pattern after they hit the bricks of the lower terrace.

She watched Walter welcome the downpour with outspread arms and his face tilted skyward. He twirled about through the falling water without care, the sun now so clearly confined for hours. She could see his skin through the soaked cloth of his shirt, and his wet shorts clung to the contours of his body and his bangs covered his eyebrows. He looked right at her, inviting her even as he knew she couldn't accept, or wouldn't.

Barbara motioned to come share her cover. Walter lowered his cocked brow and smiled oddly, to ask without words if she was crazy.

"Bye!" Walter shouted, waving, running down the hill. He slipped and fell and tumbled a short distance, got up laughing, twirled again and more, then continued on down.

Across the years the intersections of Barbara and Roger

had eroded into habit. Dented and cracked by the loss of Bradley, the wan marriage continued on like the wrecked cars she saw the others driving, those beyond her insulation. Headlights and taillights held in place by gaffer's tape, trunk lids wired down with coat hangers. Exposed metal long rusted, a wandering, dividing crack across the windshield.

Their rooms were at opposite ends of the upstairs hall. Roger was out of the house early most mornings, rarely eating breakfast at home. She often slept 'til nine or ten or so, if not ten thirty once and again. If he had a late night she might already be in bed, and often already asleep. Two days passing without seeing one another was not unknown.

Across these years now Roger struggled to console his wife. Bradley had of course not come from his body, an experience of one gender beyond any link words could make with the other. He thought their life was better now – he knew so – but, right after, life was hideous. Waking up each new day held the task, once again, of figuring ways to not acknowledge what needed acknowl-edging. On some days he saw infinity in her eyes.

And so he placated her with things, stuff which she accepted simply to please him. The hole of Bradley had been detoured around by both, as if orange cones marked their tragedy and his absence. Young death, especially, knocks survivors from known and familiar footings, shoving those lives to new tangents that diverge like that windshield crack. She had to believe their life together was more than play acting, and she did believe so.

She often did not dream, or did not remember the dreaming, but now Walter catalyzed her dream state. He was in them. Some mornings she awoke before dawn to find herself thinking of the boy. He told her she was pretty and in her lizard brain she believed him and in her lizard brain she thanked him and in her lizard brain she waited for him.

On those still-night mornings she remembered him in the rain. She wondered had he been alone that day would he have thrown off his clothes to be naked in the wet. In her luxury, her time so terribly unclaimed by others, she recalled the near transparency of his wet T-shirt, his skin beneath and visible, his chest not so much one of a boy anymore, the features of his face that should have been disjointed but were not. His cotton shorts were nearly as light in weight as his shirt, not quite as transparent. In that rain the fabric clung to his buttocks and outlined his loins and told of no underwear and she wondered if maybe he was thirteen or fourteen after all and she wondered more what he would be in ten years. Or five. Or maybe two.

On many days of that second summer, after his solstice

appearance, Barbara would spend mornings, afternoons reading on the lower terrace, looking up occasionally to scan the woods. She cut Loraine back to two days, and then one, although she continued to pay her for three. Clearly, Walter's visits required not only summer and clouds, but her solitude. Yet despite her being alone so much of the summer Walter had not returned. The equinox nearly at hand, this light-balanced day would be a final bookend for this year. Maybe forever, she feared.

On a few scattered nights, when Roger was late, she scanned for Walter, although he had never come in any kind of darkness. Still, though. Owls lived in the woods, hoot-hoot-hooting. Bats performed abstract ballets as they hunted insects in midair. On some of those clear nights she would see a meteor ignite as it passed through the atmosphere. Their suburban setting, sparse and private, allowed stars and constellations to bloom as dusk became night.

On any night fireflies by the many hundreds dotted the trees from their crowns to their lowest branches. Their flashes were random, of course. Completely. But then what if they were not? What if, all together, from a certain distance and a certain parallax, the flashes held a message? They seemed to be a Morse code of nature, dot dash, dot dot dash. Or if not a direct message, then perhaps simply a meaning to be had in some way or another. Or maybe, yes, a message from Walter. Or about him, for Walter and the woods seemed bonded in some way that expressed itself empirically, and only empirically, with no hypothesis identifiable.

Despite scanning and looking during the early afternoon of the equinox, the cottonwoods already shedding leaves, the warm nights of summer mostly gone, she didn't see Walter until he was halfway up the hill. "Walter!" she announced. He smiled fully and waved to her. As he approached she told, "I thought I'd never see you again. The summer's over and I thought—"

"Not quite over. And you were always going to see me again," he told as fact. In her reticence and propriety she had denied herself embracing Walter during his visits, if only in a motherly way, and still even now maintained that denial against her yearning. "It's warm today, not many clouds right now. But I needed to come, you see." From the west storm clouds were advancing quickly, but presently above existing clouds were thinning. "But then I must go. Soon."

"Well, look now, please come in. It's cool inside, you know."

"No. I can't." He took half a step back, then moved to stand under the umbrella. For several minutes the sun was in more show, but then the huge sailing cumulo-nimbus clouds moving east began erasing the shadows again. "I really must go. While I can."

"But look," she said pointing upward. "There's no shadow now. And there won't be."

"No. But now isn't about shadows. Now is about leaving soon."

"But you only just arrived. You're going? So quickly?"

"Yes."

"But you said I was always going to see you again!"

"And you have."

"But … well I mean, not, not after this time, I just know. This time right now. Not again. I'll never see you again." Her eyes welled, so unlike her. "I *know* I'll never see you again. Ever."

"That … is up to you," he smiled. "There is a time, Barbara. Right now. And it's closing."

"Closing?" she pleaded. He answered with a look that told her questions were pointless. *Dear God, oh my dearest God this errant man boy, without thought or expectation or reason, has made my world bearable.* A ghost in her proper machine. An awakening about her and across her and within her. A hope to perhaps be touched by living or just life. Walter extended his right hand, not to shake hers in goodbye but as an invitation.

She looked up with welcoming eyes at the clouds and the rain they promised. The clouds were now unbroken into the west, offering long cover. Oh, and was she weary of living? Or of this present life and plane, anyway. Anyway, a life with unseen death and of the apartness from the shards of it. Without Bradley they became strangers even as they grasped for one another in murk. Each was not at fault as much as each was at fault, for Death can weaken sheer holding on beyond all human will. Little had been salved by silk and leather and silver and gold. Not by German engineering or haute cuisine or square footage for the sake of mere bigness. Temporary relief evaporating could be worse than no relief, she had found.

She took two steps to reach his hand, then accepted his slender fingers around her own. Touching him, at last. A brief, slight shudder shot through her, a current then repeating as she again remembered him wet and dancing and so much a part of something she was not.

In Barbara's subconscious mind were facts, of course, observable facts. Across a year and another summer Walter hadn't changed. He had grown no taller, he did not weigh one pound more, nor had his voice ever changed or even his clothes. But when these truths surfaced like arcing whales into her fully conscious mind they were denied not only meaning, but acknowledgement.

Walter spotted Roger's Mercedes along the road to

nowhere, approaching the house. He grasped her fingers firmly now. Too firmly, almost, yet only almost.

As he led her down the sloping lawn towards the creek and the waiting woods visceral memories of childhood colored her mind and challenged time. Slow and distant thunder was heard, of the sort not violent but suggesting of pillows in the sky. She saw a curtain of rain move from the forest and up the hill, soon to include them. The nascent fear she knew just then was not focused, and so was also electric and held glimmering appeal. The questions she found in Bradley's room were forgotten, or maybe answered. She knew once across she would never breach the creek again and she accepted this knowledge as if simply taking in another breath.

With purpose carried in their mutual gait the two began their climb up the wooded slope. At once she felt a welcoming aether about her, nearly too welcoming she might have understood had her subjugation, just right then, been not so delicious, so delicate.

After lunch that day Roger found himself, spontaneously and delightfully, in high spirits. He was coming home early to surprise Barbara with his own invitation to an evening of whatever his wife fancied, simply any whim or lark at all! He walked through the house calling Barbara's name happily, continuing to the doors leading to the upper terrace. He looked through the rain across the lawn, then across the creek and up into the woods. He thought he saw his wife and another figure walking up the slope. In his concern he fumbled about to open a door. Then in the rain he inhaled air enough to power a mighty shout through cupped hands, but then stopped his summons short, wondering now if he had seen her, or anyone, at all.

You Can't Miss It

There's an Arby's across the federal highway from the Crossmoor Real Estate Offices. I must drive the one tenth of one mile there, of course, or risk becoming human road kill on and in the brush guard of an H2 Hummer driven by a cell-yakking lacrosse mom with an Hermes scarf stuffed under the passenger seat like a couple of empty baked-pie boxes from McDonald's. One apple, one cherry. Sixty in a forty-five because she's special and important. Or late for her facial, anyway.

I sometimes like the Arby's and its anonymity. Sure, sometimes one particular manager affects folksy familiarity with me, but the large eating area beyond the counter typically finds just a scant lot of a half dozen solitary and glum faces in search of Edward Hopper. The kid who took my order yesterday got on his cell soon after, and I pretty much figured he was talking to his parole officer, who, given the kid's defensive answers, wasn't all that happy, I guess.

Anyway, yesterday I was eating a cherry turnover with a hairpin road of white icing. The pastry comes as a right triangle and as I began to chomp on one of the 45s I felt twelve for a moment, and I've reached some sort of life nexus at which I need to feel twelve again. Or want to anyway. So I'm eating the turnover yesterday when I realize I've been at Crossmoor exactly one year. Interestingly, no one had said whoop about it, including me, if just to myself.

This is surprising, though, this milestone. Sure, I stuck with getting my license, mostly online, and I did receive recognition for my mastery of the Crossmoor training program, mostly K-Mart psychology. Still, I figured I'd be fired or quit during the first week after training. Ten days max. But I was not and had not, and this was curious, sort of, except at times I had actually made some almost serious money, which I had not expected to do. Frankly, across a work history jagging from freshman English instructor to fire spotter to assistant earthen dam inspector I had never vaguely approached almost serious money. But now I had … well, close enough to spit on it. And I liked that prospect.

And there was Abby. No, not Arby's, Abby. So I stayed.

Not that Abby and I are involved in any angle beyond Platonic. Well, not even that, really. She says she is married, has a ring. So I guess she is, although in just what way isn't clear, given she never comes forth with mention of husband or issue. Not that there is a zap between us. There isn't. It's just that I connect with her because she is so unlike every real estate sales agent I've ever met, including, of course, every Crossmoor agent beyond the set of Abby and me. None of the others is **FABULOUS INSIDE!** but Abby is, really, in a scientific and logical way that is both refreshing and reassuring.

Abby had initiated and negotiated a buyout from her job at OmniUni Chemical before her boss could find cause to can her fifty-five-year-old butt. She seems, at first, quite unlikely as a real estate sales person, but maybe her inability to bullshit buyers and sellers is poetic justice in motion, considering she has become a top seller. She is no-nonsense because she has no nonsense. She is thorough and professional and knows how to move a deal along proactively – like a catalyst in a chemical reaction, I guess – and she's getting seven-figure listings now, which means thirty- and forty-thousand dollar commissions. Sometimes such a fancy listing will run six months or better, that's true, but right at the start the stratospheric price tends to vet pretty well the amateur posers, the wannabes without nerve and the generally unqualified. The deal is, apparently a lot of people read a *for sale* sign as *free entertainment*. Go figure.

"You're showing the Peterson house at 2:00?" Abby asks,

almost rhetorically but not quite. She knows I am, since she has, somehow, finagled this top listing to me, my first. Just about all of the past year I acknowledged silently at Arby's yesterday was spent splitting commissions on starter homes and sometimes dealing with short sales. Two, three grand. Sometimes just fifteen or even twelve hundred from a commission split on weedy little houses smack on the other side of town from the Peterson house. Quietly desperate places on slabs with the square footage of some present-day master suites and an eight-foot chain link fence along the rear property line with a two-acre drainage project holding basin beyond, the tool shed next door a possible meth lab. Sure, there were scattered pieces o' cake, but most of my sales had involved many days of long hours and many dozens of gallons of gasoline and countless phone calls from the anxious and the barely qualified and the generally inept.

"Yep. To the Turtlesons."

"Turlsons. Don't screw the pooch. Not this one anyway."

"Right. Got it. TURL-son." I have already met the Turtle—er, Turlsons, at the Taylor's open house a Sunday or two back. I did not like them, and presently I do not like both equally. He wore a yellow cravat embroidered with tiny Irish Setters and she pushed a half dozen lemon cookies wrapped in a napkin into her purse while dressed like Betty Ford, circa the early post-resignation days. He complained the jambs were not fluted and she lamented the floors were too random in width. Boo frickin' hoo.

Before they introduced themselves I could tell somehow his name was William – he just looked like one, you know? – and I had a hunch he used the whole enchilada, although I did give *Liam* 9-1 odds, but I guess he didn't imagine himself as that faux landed. Her name was Sueellen, and about her moniker she explained quickly and explicitly it was a single word, not Sue Ellen. Really? In print the name looked vaguely exotic, perhaps French African. Yet when spoken by her in her fake and nasally Tidewater accent, and in her rush to squish three syllables into two and a half in order to further extend the peculiar single-word expression of her ordinary name and so making it come out *Swellen*, I was reminded of the viral hemorrhagic fevers. They drove up in one of those retro-looking Jaguars.

Last Sunday they had laughed openly if quietly at the Taylor's Mondrian above the living room mantel. It's genuine, if you care, and as long as we're at it he's one of my favorites. I figure the Turlsons, if they're still screwing, do so like a reciprocating steam engine and I will bet anyone a grand right now they've never banged in daylight or with the lights on. I can tell.

The Peterson house lists for nine hundred twenty-five thousand dollars US. The Turlsons seem to have some kind of jack, I will give 'em that. Given their late forties to mid-fifties age range somebody must've died and there was an inheritance and now they're hoping to make up for their lost years in the wrong zip code. Anyway, they're driving that nouveau Inspector Morse Jag and they weren't pre-qualified because they're paying cash, which he confirmed voluntarily with an ATM savings account balance slip on which was printed this: Available balance $1,132,016.77. And they don't flinch at this nearly mil price tag, and by that I mean I'm allowing myself to salivate over the possibility the duo might pay asking price. True, the Peterson's house is a faithful Tudor to the extent of noteworthiness in a terribly proper location, situated on a half-acre lot of matured planting and in pretty good original condition. Five bedrooms, three full bathrooms and two half baths, two fireplaces down and one in the master suite, slate roof, what was originally a maid's quarters above the garage and a gardener's toilet off the garage. Snazzy! But it needs easily one hundred fifty K of updates regarding not only systems' efficiency but the pacification of the granite countertop, Sub Zero, shit-don't-smell crowd. You know, the babe in the Hummer who's never boiled an egg atop her Vulcan restaurant cooker. Actually, lets go with two hundred K.

"You need to leave, then. It's 1:30. Get going."

"Right! On my way." The Crossmoor policy is to arrive twenty minutes early if the house is occupied and ten if vacant. I climb into my '01 Oldsmobile Intrigue. A welcomed gift from my Aunt Phoebe one week before she happened to die anyway, bless he heart. As her life had gone, she had clocked 16,307 miles in eight years of driving to the grocery store and doctors' offices, of motoring to luncheons and matinees and meetings of bird watchers, and as a hospital volunteer reading Michener to sick people. A sweet ride. Sweet enough for me, anyway.

I arrive at 1:50. The Turlsons aren't there, but Mr. Peterson is and that's bad, and I know had I arrived at 1:40 it would still be bad. I wouldn't hesitate to tell any other client, very politely, to skedaddle … but not Mr. Peterson. He's a truly great guy who has lived in this house fifty-one years, raised four kids in it and buried his wife and one of those kids from it. And here he is, reminiscing in the side yard before surrendering himself to his assisted-living kennel crate. And why the hell not? He still lives here, God damn it, which is good because his furniture, rugs and doodads are very fine and accentuate the house and the potential lifestyle of a potential buyer. Potentially.

Billy and Ebola ring up my cell. "I thought you said turn right onto Glenwood," she queries accusatively and without a hello.

"Oh I'm so sorry, Mrs. Turlson. What I –"

"WHAT?"

"I'm sorry?"

"Did you say *Turtleson*? I think you said *Turtleson*. You did!"

"Why, no, Mrs. Turlson," I offer honestly, although maybe in subconscious rabblerousing I had let it slip. "It must be my connection."

"Uh-huh. Yeah. Look, how the hell do we get to this house?"

"Where are you now, Mrs. Turlson?"

"Where are we, William? Huh? Oh. Sussex Place."

"Just go back to Kensington Boulevard. Go east, towards town, and turn left onto Woodglen. The Peterson house is at Woodglen and Pineloch. You can't miss it."

"Hold on," she orders. Then in the background I hear, "GPS Wooded Glen and Pinelot, William. He says we can't miss it. Yeah right."

"It's, it's Wood*glen*, Mrs. Turlson. W-O-O-D-G-L-E-N, one word. And It's Pine*loch*. P-I-N-E-L-O-C-H."

"Huh? Well that spells Pine-loach."

"It's pronounced *lock*, Mrs. Turlson. It's Gaelic, I would think."

There is no direct response, then, "OK, we got it." CLICK.

If I can't get Mr. Peterson to hang back, this particle collision will, quite probably, turn ugly. You know, matter, anti-matter … the null set. The Peterson's is an exclusive listing with Crossmoor, so we're talking a twenty-seven K and change commission in my pocket. When Billy showed me his savings account balance I couldn't help thinking of my own of $122.37.

Mr. Peterson had been a senior partner in a top law firm in one of the downtown bank towers. The main door to their offices was a six-panel solid mahogany affair topped with a broken pediment, which clashed effectively with the Bauhaus nature of the building. Mr. Peterson had been one of the most potent trial lawyers in town, which of course means his acumen for human behavior is still as keen as his contemplative knowledge of, and reverence for, the law.

I start to wonder where the Turlsons might be when they turn onto the driveway and come skidding to a gravelly stop. Ebola jumps out and spits, "It's a miracle we found the place with those flapdoodle directions you gave. Can't miss it? Hah!"

"Well, I'm so very glad you did find it, Mrs. Turlson. Mr. Turlson, so nice to see you again."

"Well, yes, I, uh—" Billy begins before Ebola gives him a shut-the-hell-up look.

"Mr. Peterson, please meet Mr. and Mrs. Turlson."

"How do you—"

"I thought this was a private showing," she interrupts.

"By all means it is. Mr. Peterson is the owner."

Poor Billy attempts again, "This is a lovely ho—"

"It might do," Ebola mutters, chopping off her husband's sentence.

"Well, please come in." We walk through the front door.

As I point out the inch-thick oak floors and the boxed ceilings and the leaded windows with the stained-glass centers I become aware of Mr. Peterson following us quietly, staying out of sight in the previous room. His shadowing is a better scenario than I had hoped for and makes the showing workable.

The Turlsons show no enthusiasm. What follows is a sample of the two's reactions to their tour of the Peterson home:

"Well, we could always pickle the paneling and ceiling in the study. That might make it less dreary," she says.

"It's not at all clear to me the floors are level," he says.

"Those bathrooms look like time machines," she says.

"Ya think bats are in the attic?" he wonders.

"The kitchen cabinets are older than we are. In fact, that entire kitchen is an absolute *disaster* site," she says.

"Yes," he says, and then with a hollow little laugh adds, "Perhaps we could get FEMA to pay for it."

"Oh that's good, William. Very good. Isn't it?" she asks, turning to me.

"Oh, yes, quite. So clever, Mr. Turlson." As I stop myself from muttering *you should be on the New York stage* I turn around quickly to glance, perhaps, Mr. Peterson, and do. To my betrayal he simply smiles with closed lips and gives a quick wave.

As the tour continues so do the Turlson's criticisms. The basement "seems to have an odd aroma." The screened porch "could be enclosed for an exercise room." And then their final, heartless salvo:

- We'll need to get bids on replacement windows

- What is that, a slate roof? Who would have that?

- Maybe we'll paint the entire house off, off white. You know, taupe. Or bisque.

Billy then brushes away my afternoon's efforts with a dismissive, "We'll think about it." *Yeah, Billy Bob Turlson* I think *you do that. Hope you enjoyed your free entertainment. Why don't you dig out a two-for-one coupon from Swellen's purse and have yourself a late lunch at Applebee's.*

Billy, Ebola and I exit through the service entrance and walk across the terrace to near the garage. Then I hear the approaching steps of Mr. Peterson as he follows us outside. Mr. Peterson, with a professional lifetime of reading people as they gave depositions or delivered testimony in court. Mr. Peterson, who knew the diametric pull of defending the guilty because it was his duty. Good ol' Henry Peterson knows full well the Turlson's are in such vampire-like pursuit of perceived heritage and lineage they will change little beyond the outdated kitchen. He has a good hunch that, like it or not, these cretins are the most likely buyers to come through in forty days, and now it's just business.

As I turn to meet his steps I see a man suddenly not so much in need of assistance in living. He walks up to the pair, although more to Billy. "Listen here, Big Lord Fauntleroy," Mr. Peterson declares, "you wouldn't know white oak from white pine if it bit you in the ass. And by the way, that thing you drove up in is not a Jaguar, it's a Ford. This," he continues, pointing a remote at the garage, "is a Jaguar." And behold, as the right-hand door lifts the toothy grille of a 1959 MK II, in utter and total pristine condition, is revealed. "You can't have my house. I will not allow that car, that ... imposter, to be parked in my garage. I will not sell my home to the likes of you. Never!"

There is only silence. The Crossmoor prep course failed to cover the last stand of Henry Peterson, leaving me with a mouth open but no words exiting. But then the nothingness is filled by the hissing of Billy.

"Oh really. Let me tell you something, bub, you have to sell us your house. You can't *not* sell it to any qualified buyer. And guess what?" Billy smirks, "We're qualified as hell. Cold cash on the frickin' barrelhead qualified." Then he turns to me to demand, with a sneering contempt that would make up for the fact I was never on Nixon's enemies list, "What is the price of—"

Ebola can no longer contain herself. "William! Let's not jump—"

"I'll handle this, Swellen. Nine hundred twenty-five thousand dollars. That right?" he asks, looking directly at me.

"It is," I squeak out.

He turns to Mr. Peterson, "Loose change, pal. Not a second thought about it from William Elslington Turlson. That's me." Then spinning back to me, "Do you have the papers to sign?"

"Yes, sir. I'll get them."

"I'll write the deposit check while you do. Will fifty thousand be sufficient?"

I walk quickly to my car, almost tripping on the root of a maple. Returning with the papers, Billy grabs them. There is an awkward sequence of *here, and here, and initial here*, during which time Mr. Peterson slips away.

With all lines signed Billy hands the check to me and demands, "I'll wait to watch you place the *sold* sign, if you don't mind."

"I, uh, I didn't bring one. But it'll be up—"

"Didn't think so," he smirks victoriously. "Didn't think there'd be one in the trunk of your *Olds*mobile. What's it like to drive a marque nobody wanted ten years ago? You weren't prepared. I am." Then he and Ebola climb into their past-evoking Jaguar and speed away as the new owners of 201 Pineloch Road.

I watch their car get smaller, then continue to look in the general direction of their departure even after they have turned the corner, flapping about for enough minutes to convince myself that what has just happened, really has. I even allow myself to imagine my upcoming savings account balance of $27,872.37.

Mr. Peterson walks from the shadows of the garage, and then up to me with a twinkle and a wink. "You owe me one," he says.

Also by Fairleigh Brooks

Fiction

Mr. Willy & Arthur

An imagined meeting between two of the most iconic characters in American literature, Boo Radley and Willy Loman. The author changes time and fates for both men – just a little for Willy, a great deal for Boo. The result is an intersection of desperation and perseverance.

Notes of a Would-Be Astronaut

"An engaging inner and outer travelogue, replete with vivid descriptions, vignettes of fascinating characters, and inner knots reminiscent of R.D. Laing. This story of

Passages-midlife crisis search for self is sure to resonate with many of us, especially those who like to think while they read. Enjoy!"

– Stan Franklin, author of Artificial Minds

A Presentation of Short Stories Without Regard to Marketing

Lady Chatterley's Pool Boy

Nonfiction

Beyond 17: The Apollo Applications Program and Losing the New Frontier (2023)

About the Author

Fairleigh Brooks is an author, essayist, and a former commentator for NPR affiliate WFPL in Louisville, Kentucky. In addition to his novels and literary collections, his short story "Washing Dishes" was published in the literary journal *Arable* and another, "Miles From the Edge, Years From the End" was published in *Tobacco, a Literary Anthology*. Brooks also writes about the history of science and technology, focused largely on space exploration, specifically manned space exploration. Within these considerations Brooks has explored how technology arose, its purpose, and how technology changes the ideas and concepts of who we are, and why we are.

Wordsmith on LinkedIn

Topics from popular culture to architecture to civil rights to Charlie Brown's Christmas.